FOOTFALLS CAME FROM BEHIND.

I've got to create a distraction, Mike told himself. *Think.* Suddenly, he was dancing and hopping and banging his tail crazily on the ground. "Wugga-wugga-wugga!" he hollered.

The giant T. rex in front of him froze. It stared at him as if he'd gone mad. The footfalls behind him stopped, too. His distraction had worked on both T. rexes!

This was Mike's chance. He raced for the shoreline.

"Come on in, ya big wussbags, the water's fine!" Mike shouted as he entered the waves. The big rex grunted. His companion grunted. But neither would move into the water.

"Wimps! Wussies!" Mike shouted. Then he felt it.

Suddenly, he understood why they hadn't followed. He was sinking. It was because he weighed so much! Tons!

The beach was swallowing him up, like quicksand...

**The adventure continues
in these other DINOVERSE titles
by Scott Ciencin**

**#2 The Teens Time Forgot
#3 Raptor Without a Cause
#4 Please Don't Eat the Teacher!**

*It's time to figure out
when to live by your wits...
and when to trust your instincts.*

I WAS A TEENAGE T. REX

by Scott Ciencin

illustrated by Mike Fredericks

RANDOM HOUSE 🏠 NEW YORK

To my beloved wife, Denise.
This novel is as much a part
of her heart and soul as it is mine.
—S.C.

Text copyright © 1999 by Scott Ciencin
Interior illustrations © 1999 by Mike Fredericks
Cover art © 1999 by Adrian Chesterman

www.randomhouse.com/kids

Library of Congress Catalog Card Number: 99-67537
ISBN: 0-679-88843-8
RL: 5.5

Cover design by Georgia Morrissey
Interior design by Gretchen Schuler

Printed in the United States of America   March 2000   10 9 8 7 6 5 4 3 2 1

Dear Reader,

If you're like me, you love dinosaurs. Maybe you've also imagined what it would be like to look through their eyes and listen through their ears.

With the help of paleontologist Dr. Thomas R. Holtz, Jr., I was able to take a journey back in time to live with these amazing creatures. Unlike Bertram Phillips, I didn't have access to a time machine to travel back 67 million years, so I did the next best thing. I read as much about dinosaurs as I could. What I learned about how they lived, what they ate, and what their world was like I placed in this series of adventures I call DINOVERSE.

You can take your own trip back in time, too. The library has plenty of books about dinosaurs, and more are written every day. The Internet is always buzzing with up-to-the-minute information on new finds. Documentaries and television shows about dinosaur discoveries are constantly being produced.

Best of all, you won't ever have to settle for just one opinion about anything concerning dinosaurs. Paleontologists often find different ways of looking at things, and that leaves room for you to become a paleo-detective yourself. Check out what they've found, and form your own ideas.

But you'd better look sharp while you're digging around in the past because you could get lost back there. Of course, if you do, you might just have the time of your life. I sure did!

Scott Ciencin

Psst! Check out Bertram's dino notebook on page 171!

And his favorite dino Web sites on page 177!

PROLOGUE

Wetherford, Montana
Late September

The day he'd been waiting for finally arrived.

Bertram Phillips glanced at the wooden dinosaur clock his dad had made. The big hand was on the Icarosaurus, the little hand on the Afrovenator. That meant it was ten past seven, and Doc Phillips—as his dad liked to be called—was late. *Way* late.

Frowning, Bertram rose from the breakfast table, where he had spent the last hour laying out a special *feast* in honor of the big day. He stuck the cookbooks back on the shelf and braced them with his dad's Velociraptor bookends. He opened the oven and used the "Bucky the Brontosaurus" mitts to take out the croissants—his dad's favorite—before they burned.

Then he left the kitchen, walking past the text-books and paleontology magazines that were stacked in every room. Since he was alone so much, Bertram had read many of these books. In fact, he knew pretty much everything about the Mesozoic, what paleontologists—and grad students like his dad—called the era of the dinosaurs.

When he reached his dad's bedroom, Bertram rapped on the door with the replica Nanotyrannus jawbone knocker. No reply.

"Um...Dad?" Bertram called. "Dad, it's time to get going!"

Bertram was used to his dad's never showing up on time for anything. Mom had been the only one who could keep Doc Phillips on schedule. But Bertram and his dad had been on their own for a while now, so no matter how much Bertram set the clocks forward, it was never enough.

Bertram knocked again. His dad wasn't answering him. Weird. He opened the door and stepped inside.

Bertram's gaze went right to the bed. A note sat beside a heap of wrinkled white sheets in the middle of the mattress.

Bertram's heart sank as he picked up the note and read:

> Yo, Claw-Brother!
>   I just picked up an e-mail about a breakthrough on the site. It's around three in the morning now, and I'm going to check it out with Bobo and Finch. It looks like we might have a pelvis bone from some kind of super-

predator, something bigger than T. rex, bigger than Giganotosaurus, too!

 I know you have your science fair today,
and I'll do my best to be there. Later, you
little troglodyte.

                                          —Doc

Bertram swallowed. He forced away the sting in
his eyes and throat, but a dead weight remained in
his chest.

There'd been no mention of his birthday. None.
Worst of all, the note had been signed "Doc." Just
once he'd like to find a note signed "Dad."

Putting the note aside, Bertram left the room and
plodded down the steps. "He'll be there," he whispered, collecting his books. "He'll be there..."

As he waited for the school bus, Bertram adjusted his thick glasses. At thirteen, he was small for his age and a little round in places he wished he wasn't. He had brown hair and was a "good-looking boy," or so his relatives told him whenever they visited. Which wasn't very often. Today, he wore his favorite outfit: a deep blue V-neck sweater with a powder blue shirt beneath, khaki pants, and earth-tone shoes.

A couple of neighborhood kids circled the wide street on their bikes. One of them noticed Bertram and yelled, "Hey, it's Blurtrum, the intelligent idiot!"

"No!" called another. "It's Bert-RAM—he's got a computer for a brain."

While the first two were taunting him, another let out a bloodcurdling cry and sped his bike right at him. Bertram drew back from the charge in alarm. His attacker cut the wheel and blurred past.

A sudden flash flood of mud and gunk rose up, splattering Bertram from head to foot. He hadn't even noticed the puddle by the curb. His tormentors cackled, then took off in search of other prey.

"Predators," Bertram muttered. He went back in the house, showered, and changed into a plaid shirt—white T beneath—and his *other* pair of khaki pants and earth-tone shoes. By then, the bus had come and gone.

He walked to school, arriving late. He was surprised to see lines of students outside. The closest line was made up of kids from his homeroom. One of them, Mike Peterefsky, waved.

Mike was tall, handsome, with strong cheekbones, warm blue eyes, and a friendly smile. His brownish blond hair was cut in the same style as most of the football players'. It was short, spiky on top, and shaved a little on the sides. As usual, he wore torn, baggy jeans and his older brother's varsity jacket. Beneath the jacket was a Tigger T-shirt.

A few of Mike's friends groaned as Bertram approached. One of them, Sean O'Malley, glared. Sean was the tallest guy in their entire junior high, and Mike's only real competition for the title of star football player. Sean had a little scar on his chin. His eyes were small, mean, and glacier gray. Today he wore a tank top that showed off his muscular arms and shoulders, and he acted as if the cold didn't bother him.

Bertram froze.

"Come on," Mike said. He gestured for Bertram to come closer. Next to him, Sean shook his head and turned away, smacking Mike with his shoulder.

Mike looked at his teammate and buddy. "What?"

"Survival of the fittest. Remember that."

Mike frowned as Sean drifted farther up in line. Bertram moved closer, and Mike put his hands on Bertram's shoulders, then guided him into line ahead of him.

"Ms. Carol's gone to see why we haven't been let

back in by now," Mike explained.

"Yeah, but I'm late," Bertram said. "I've gotta get a pass and—"

"You leave that to me," Mike promised.

Bertram knew he could trust Mike. Still, there was something odd in Mike's eyes. He seemed troubled. Bertram wondered what was wrong. He gestured at the line and said, "So what's going on?"

"It's either a fire drill or a false alarm."

"*Or* the real thing," a female voice cut in.

Bertram looked up suddenly. He nearly choked. The prettiest girl in the eighth grade was looking over from another line. Candayce Chambers.

"I mean, we can hope, right?" Candayce said.

Bertram gasped. He always gasped when she was near. Candayce was radiant. Naturally blond hair trailed midway down her back, elegantly styled as always. A tan from her summer vacation in Florida. Rosy cheeks. Perfect teeth. Glittering green eyes.

Next to her was Tanya Call. Tanya's red beaded tank top exposed her temporary mehndi tattoos.

"How ya doin', ladies?" Mike asked.

Candayce absently brushed something from the shoulder of her pretty green-and-aqua blouse. "Looking forward to this geeky science fair thingee."

"Really?" Bertram asked. His heart rose.

The dark-haired Tanya leaned forward. "It gets us out of class, nimsey-doodle."

"Right," Bertram said. He looked down at his shoes, knowing they weren't geek shoes but feeling as if they were, since *he* had them on.

Then Candayce straightened her cloud-print skirt, and Bertram stared, feeling himself getting lost in those clouds. He hauled his gaze to her emerald eyes and watched as she confidently tossed her hair.

Spotting one of her rivals, Candayce frowned. Her serene, heavenly expression turned to pure evil. Bertram knew it was time for Dish 101.

"Look, there's Plastica!" Candayce said, loud enough to make sure she was heard.

Tanya joined in. "Hey, Pam! Nice nose job!"

Their victim scurried away, throwing nervous glances over her shoulder while she cupped her hand over her nose. Mike sighed disapprovingly, but Candayce had gone into Terminator mode. She would *not* be stopped.

"Did you know she wears butt pads?" Candayce asked.

"Are you kidding me?" Tanya replied with predatory interest.

"About something like that? No way. And I saw little Miss Wombeley in the girls' shower the other day. Stretch marks *and* cellulite. Guess where."

Bertram tried to tune out what they were saying, but it was impossible. Candayce was the prettiest girl he'd ever seen, a goddess on the outside—but within, she was a carnivore. That particular knowledge was among the saddest he'd ever acquired.

"Oh, God," Candayce said. She covered her face with one hand. *"Major* loser alert."

Bertram looked up and saw Janine Farehouse approaching. She was short, with a stocky, compact little rectangle of a body, black hair she seldom did anything with, and dark, knowing eyes that never missed a thing—though you wouldn't know that from the way she almost always seemed to be looking somewhere else. She was pretty, though Bertram knew better than to ever say that to her face. He tried not to even think it in her presence.

Janine wore a flannel shirt, blue jeans, and black boots. Her heavy key chain *chonked* and *chinged* as she walked by. She held it by the steel wolf head and flicked her keys on their long chain. Behind her was a teacher, Mr. Graves, hands on his hips, gaze cast down at his own lengthening shadow, head shaking violently from side to side.

Bertram instantly guessed that Janine had been blamed for the fire alarm—and that she had talked her way out of it.

"Oh, look, it's the girl most likely to be living alone with five cats by the time she's twenty," Candayce muttered.

"I wish *I* could spend all my spare time changing sheets," Tanya added.

Bertram frowned. Janine's mom ran the Autumn's

Fest bed-and-breakfast on the outskirts of town. Janine spent most of her time there or at school. Or getting into trouble.

Janine stopped and looked at the pair of girls. Candayce and Tanya tried to look tough, but each of them took a step back. Janine seemed to be doing more than looking at them. She was looking *inside* them. Making them shrivel. Words weren't necessary.

Smiling, Janine moved on, disappearing behind another line of students.

"How do you ward off the evil eye again?" Candayce muttered, trying to make a strange symbol with her hand and fingers.

"No, like this, like *this*," Tanya said.

Ms. Carol came to their line. She looked pretty distracted, even before she spotted Bertram.

Mike stepped forward. "Yeah, I was wondering why you didn't count Bertram present before. He raised his hand and everything."

"Oh," Ms. Carol said absently. "Um...sorry, right..." She turned. "Okay, class, it was a false alarm. They'll be letting us back in anytime now."

Bertram turned to Mike. "Thanks."

Mike shrugged. "It's nothing."

But it was *something* to Bertram. Mike's simple gesture of friendship had meant the world to him.

By the time the students were let back in, it was twenty minutes after eight. Bertram was excused so he could go to the science fair. He got to the gym and made his way through the various exhibits until he came to the small tent Mr. London had helped him set up two nights before. Excited with anticipation, he slipped inside the tent and surveyed his masterpiece.

Bertram's M.I.N.D. Machine, his Memory INterpreter Device, was a fabulous contraption. It stretched ten feet across, was eight feet high, and went back six feet. Dozens of computer screens were embedded in its mishmashed mess of a face. Cables as thick as a man's arm and corrugated metal sleeves connected one mechanism to another.

At its center was a used office chair that had been cleverly remade as the Launch Seat. A pair of joysticks and rows of push-button controls adorned the arms. A canopy of gadgets sat over the headrest, with little wires and suction cups dangling from them.

Bertram smiled. He'd seen many of the other exhibits. They were nothing compared to his masterpiece. So what if it was all an illusion?

Nearly every component in his machine was there just for show. At its heart was a simple biofeedback machine and a single functioning home computer. The PC was equipped with a CD-ROM that would feed images to the center monitor depending on what impulses were sent through the biofeedback sensor.

The other computer screens, scavenged from junkyards and the garbage cans of computer stores across three counties, had been rigged with monofilaments that would light up like Christmas tree lights, blinking and changing patterns—but not really doing anything.

Bertram had wired and welded together a towering edifice of motherboards and circuitry panels, discarded chips and cracked disks that amounted to nothing more than a magic trick. But then, he'd learned all too well that appearance is everything. Adults liked to tell him it wasn't. But in his experience, it was.

Bertram frowned. He couldn't shake the feeling that the machine still needed something. But what?

Then it came to him. He pushed his collar back, pulled out his silver chain, and carefully removed his good-luck charm. It was a tiny T. rex bone his dad had found at their current site. Bertram opened a panel, slipped the charm inside, and sealed it again. He felt better. Now he knew the machine had every chance of working. Even his dad would be impressed.

Bertram could hear students being let into the gym. The tent flap rustled, and Mr. London appeared. The science teacher had a receding hairline and sharp, hawklike features. But his stern looks were balanced by a warm smile and a good sense of humor. Today, he wore a white shirt and a Coca-Cola Bears tie.

"Ready for the big day?" he asked.

Bertram nodded eagerly.

"Then let's take this tent down and get to business."

From somewhere close, a booming voice

announced, "I am the Great and Mighty Groz!"

Bertram took a peek at the exhibit at the next table. He saw a fortune-telling machine with a light sensor. Kids passed their hands over a violet ball, and a model of a wizard made pronouncements.

"Ask me your questions and I will reveal your destiny!" Groz gloated.

"Is Karl a doofus?" a boy asked.

Bertram heard the wizard answer, "You betcha!" Kids roared with laughter.

Bertram snickered. *This* was the competition? He had nothing to worry about.

Bertram hit a switch on the generator, kicking in the power supply. A low, rumbling *thummm* sounded. Lights blinked. Digital arrays raced back and forth. Strange images formed on the computer screens. The harsh fluorescents above dimmed for a moment. Then Bertram's M.I.N.D. Machine came to life!

A crowd gathered as Bertram and Mr. London completed the unveiling. Bertram shrank inwardly as he surveyed the sea of faces before him. He knew so many of these kids, but there was no one he could really call a friend. He looked beyond the clutch of fellow students, hoping to spot his dad, but he was nowhere to be seen.

His father's words rang hollow in his memory: *I know you have your science fair today, and I'll do my best to be there.*

"Everyone, um, hi. Thanks for coming," Bertram

said nervously. He tried to recall the lessons Mr. London had given him about public speaking, but it didn't help. He felt so nervous he thought he might pass out at any second. His head was light, and he fought a rushing wave of dizziness.

Then, in the crowd, he spotted Candayce. She wasn't saying anything. Just smiling—at him!

No, not at him. Bertram looked to a nearby window and saw Mike and a bunch of his buddies on the playing field, goofing around during their gym period with only some of their padding on. Mike caught a football, and two guys tackled him in a classic hi-lo. Bertram had read all about the various plays. He winced as Mike went down hard, then sighed with relief as the two guys got off him and Mike popped up again with the ball.

Mike was *fearless*. He could take a hit and just keep going. Bertram wished he could be like that. He also wished that Candayce would look at him the way she was looking at Mike.

Someone off to his left cleared her throat. Bertram looked over and saw Janine. She was looking right at him, right into him, and somehow it calmed him. He sensed she wasn't judging him. She understood. Understood *what*, exactly, he wasn't quite sure. But she understood, and that was enough. She winked, letting him know he should get on with it.

He nodded, then leaped into his speech. "Memories and dreams. We've all got them. For some, they're a secret thing. My machine, the Memory INterpreter Device, makes dreams a reality. It looks inside people, analyzes their memories, and shows you their dreams. So, who wants to go first? Volunteers?"

The mood among his spectators changed in a heartbeat. Suspicion replaced interest. Some kids started walking away.

"I'm not putting those sticky things on my head," Candayce said. "It'd ruin my makeup!"

Celia Brooks and her trademark Big Hat leaned over Candayce's shoulder from behind. The hat was at least a foot and a half high. "Yeah, and all the thing'd show is a blank screen."

Before Candayce could say anything, a shriek came from the audience. Joey Cirone's bare legs and boxer shorts became the center of everyone's attention as he struggled to pull up his pants.

"Joey's low-riders fell down again!" someone hollered. Everyone started laughing.

Bertram knew he had to do something. Fast. "Just to show you how safe this is, I'll go first."

He turned and wired himself into the machine. All the biofeedback device could *really* do—so far as he knew—was send a signal that would become more or less intense, depending on his brain activity. The calmer he was, the slower the pulses the machine would spit out; the more upset, the faster. Bertram had rigged the PC at the heart of the M.I.N.D. Machine to roll various images from its writable CD-ROM, depending on how slow or fast the pulses were. Fast ones got more chaotic, crazed images, like mountain goats butting heads and football players doing the same thing, and slower ones triggered images of sparkling streams, cloud formations, sunrises.

Bertram strapped himself in with a seatbelt he'd taken from an auto graveyard, then quickly applied the little black suction cups to his temples. He handed his glasses to Mr. London. His teacher smiled with what Bertram took to be genuine pride. It filled him with encouragement.

Bertram hit the remote control on the chair's arm. Trumpets sounded. Music exploded. Lights whirled. He looked into the blur that was his audience and sensed that he had them.

Bertram hit another switch and began the flow of images. He heard laughter and applause from the audience, and the occasional hushed sounds of awe. It was working!

If only he knew *which* images were being project-ed. He couldn't control that, but he could control what kind of pulses his brain was sending out. He and Mr. London had worked out a routine.

First, Bertram thought of a place he'd like to go. A secret place. In his mind, Bertram pictured the tall, strange Standing Stones from the Late Cretaceous period that had been excavated near his dad's dig. It was the very place where his dad had found the tiny T. rex bone Bertram had placed inside the machine for luck. Doc Phillips spent his weekends there with his buddies, and he sometimes let Bertram come along for their "Brew and Bones" parties.

He pictured being alone with his dad at the mysterious Standing Stones. He concentrated on the mental image. It was a peaceful waking dream. Heaven.

"Cool," someone said in the audience. Bertram smiled. He didn't know what the others were seeing on the main screen, but it had their attention.

Time for a change of pace. He decided to think about someone he admired. Someone he wished he was like. A little envy to speed up the action.

Bertram thought of Mike out on the playing field. Scoring a touchdown. Surrounded by pals. A jealous little spur formed in his heart, then was replaced by his admiration for what a decent guy Mike was. As the crowd around Bertram started cheering, thoughts of Mike faded into memories of Candayce. Her windswept hair. Glowing smile. Perfect eyes. Tingling, his heart racing, Bertram heard a bunch of guys hooting and hollering. The cheerleader reel must have gone up.

Bertram made the mistake of thinking about the things Candayce had said this morning. She was beautiful—but inside, she wasn't so pretty.

Gasps came from the audience. Bertram realized he had to get back to something more fun. He thought of Janine and wished it was possible to put what was inside her into the body of Candayce Chambers. One had the perfect body, the other the perfect soul.

Chill, Frankenweenie, he told himself. But from the oohs and aahs of the crowd, he knew he'd chosen well.

He felt a strange warmth in his body and realized he was covered in sweat. His heart was really racing now. His mind followed. What was *happening?*

Suddenly, at the edge of his vision, he saw a man approaching. *Dad?* he wondered. Bertram didn't have his glasses on and couldn't see very far. All he could tell was that the man was short and had dark hair.

"Hey, it's going too fast!" a guy shouted from the crowd. "We can't see the pictures!"

Bertram only barely registered the complaint. Fear gripped him. Something was going wrong, and his dad was going to see it! This couldn't be happening!

The M.I.N.D. Machine started shuddering. Bertram craned his neck to look at it. He squinted. Each dormant computer screen was broadcasting images. The images went past too quickly for him to make them out very well, but he had a sense that he was looking at dinosaurs. And all from the same period.

"That's...that's impossible. It doesn't make sense," he whispered. He hadn't put any images of dinosaurs on the CD. And he hadn't rigged those particular screens to show anything at all. Ninety-five percent of the machine was just junk!

Yet every single bit of the machine was in operation.

Terror overtook him. He unstrapped his seatbelt and reached for the sensors still clinging to his temples—but it was too late.

A blinding light filled his vision, and an explosion roared in his ears. Bertram was shocked to see tendrils of white flame reaching from his hands. One struck Candayce, another Janine, while a third and final bolt of rippling energy raced toward the window, where Bertram had seen Mike, and shattered it.

Bertram heard screams and the sound of breaking glass. Then he felt as if he was at the center of a tornado, being ripped and twisted away from all he knew. He was falling, tumbling, flying!

Then he was gone.

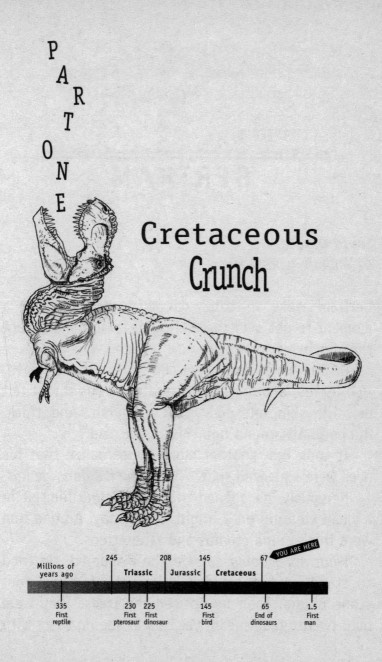

P
A
R
T

O
N
E

Cretaceous
Crunch

Millions of years ago	245		208	145		67	YOU ARE HERE
		Triassic	Jurassic	Cretaceous			

335	230	225	145	65	1.5
First reptile	First pterosaur	First dinosaur	First bird	End of dinosaurs	First man

CHAPTER 1

BERTRAM

South Dakota
67 Million Years Ago

Bertram woke in total darkness. It took him a moment to get over the feeling of falling and accept that for better or worse, he'd landed.

On his hands and knees, he smelled moist earth, rich leaves, and moss-encrusted bark. His throat felt dry. His skin felt odd. Kind of numb. And thick. Rubbery. All around him, insects buzzed.

It took him another moment to realize that his eyes were squeezed shut. *That's why it's dark, genius.*

Nervously, he opened them and found himself in a small clearing on a bright, sunny day. Around him were thick round stumps and fallen trees.

What am I doing outside? he wondered. He tried to stand up but couldn't. His limbs felt like four stone pillars. Then he noticed the trees. They were over twenty feet ahead, yet he was seeing them with perfect clarity. And he *wasn't* wearing his glasses!

Next he *identified* these particular trees. They were two-hundred-foot-tall, needle-encrusted Sequoiadendrons. In other words, they were twenty-story-high redwoods! Not the usual thing one saw in Montana. Or in the *twentieth century*.

Bertram squeezed his eyes shut again and shuddered. *This is not happening. This is not happening!*

A roar struck his ears.

Bertram opened his eyes.

He didn't see anything, but could *feel* thudding footfalls shaking the damp earth.

Whatever was making those sounds was closing in on him.

Suddenly terrified, Bertram looked for someplace to hide. His gaze locked on a beehive that hung from a redwood's limb fifty feet up. Bertram could smell the honey. Racing along a lower branch, an opossum looked for midges and beetles to eat. And Bertram could see it. Smell it. Almost *taste* it.

His senses were extraordinary!

The roar came once more. Closer this time. The footfalls were getting louder. Bertram tried again to get up—and couldn't!

He looked down at his feet. But his feet weren't there.

Instead, spaced farther apart than humanly possible, were two gray-and-orange, wrinkled, scaly boots! Except—they weren't boots. They had nails at the end of them, like an elephant's feet.

Bertram tried to move his right hand, and one of the feet stirred and came up off the ground.

Don't lose it, don't lose it, don't lose it...

Bertram's body quivered as he focused on the footprint that had been left in the earth. He now had a good idea of what had happened to him.

But *knowing* a thing and *believing* it are two different matters entirely. Bertram *knew* he was a kind of pudgy eighth grader from Montana, yet he could barely *believe* that anymore, considering the evidence to the contrary. And that evidence now included slamming, crashing footfalls coming closer.

Dead ahead, smaller trees toppled, then a dark shape appeared. A very *large* dark shape. It blocked the space between a pair of redwoods, avoiding the streaks of emerald and amber light carving their way through the dense forest.

With a roar, a towering Tyrannosaurus rex burst into the clearing. In a blur of gray-and-blue scales, the predator came charging right at Bertram. He saw the rex's huge teeth. There was no time to run.

Bertram wanted to shrink down inside himself. And that was exactly how his body responded. His torso hunkered close to the ground, his chin mashed against his chest, and his arms and legs folded up beneath him.

When the T. rex's maw came toward Bertram's

face, he squeezed his eyes shut. The rex's breath *stank*. The predator roared again, and the sound was deafening!

Bertram's backside automatically quivered. Then something attached to it rose up and slammed the ground hard enough to make the earth tremble!

Silence filled the clearing. Bertram opened his eyes and raised his head. Just a little. The T. rex came raging at him, its massive jaws snapping.

"No, no, no, no, no!" Bertram screamed as he tucked his head back down. He made his body shake and shudder until *the thing* that was attached to his backside whacked the ground again, kicking up dirt and causing the rex to jump back and away from him.

I don't like this game, Bertram thought wildly. And yet there was a part of him that *did* like it. A brave, defiant part of him knew he was tough enough to handle the rex as long as he didn't give in to the fear.

Bertram had no time to think about that *other* part of himself he'd suddenly discovered. He had to *do* something.

Okay, then. Bertram was willing to accept, for the sake of not becoming the T. rex's breakfast, that there was a reason his attacker hadn't taken a bite out of his shoulder while he cowered on the ground: *He can't. There's something there. Like armor.*

Bertram's thoughts were a whirl: Tyrannosaurus

rex. Lived sixty-five to sixty-seven million years ago. The very end of the Cretaceous period. What dinosaur could actually give a T. rex a decent battle?

An Ankylosaurus. A club-tail. *That has to be it!*

Bertram was in the past, in the body of an Ankylosaurus, and the massive spikes covering his back and head were protecting him. A good thing, too, considering he was fighting for his life!

"Can't be any worse than junior high school," he muttered.

The T. rex roared again and Bertram opened his eyes to narrow slits. He watched the Tyrannosaurus peering down at his sides, where his vulnerable belly would appear if he stood up. Bertram slapped his tail on the ground, and the rex backed off.

Whoa, Bertram thought. *He* had made a *T. rex* retreat.

Bertram allowed himself to really feel his new body for the first time. He knew that an Ankylosaurus weighed about three or four tons and that he was a plant-eater. That meant this body was all muscle. Not one ounce of fat.

Cool.

Not that he really wanted to find himself tossed back in time like this. But if it had to happen, it could have been worse. An Ankylosaurus could take care of itself. That was a lot more than Bertram had ever been able to do in the pudgy little human body he'd left behind.

How could this have happened? he wondered. *Did the M.I.N.D. Machine—?*

The T. rex roared and flew at him. Bertram realized that he'd raised his head. He tucked it down, closed his eyes, and whacked the earth with his tail. The spikes on Bertram's head prevented the predator from chomping down on him.

All right, Bertram told himself. *Think. There are only two options. Break this stalemate, or wait it out.*

As afraid as he was, he didn't think he could handle doing nothing. So he opened his eyes. Beyond the pacing, agitated T. rex was the forest.

No way out there.

Bertram would have to see the rest of the clearing. Taking a deep breath, he rose up and tried to spin himself around in a quick one-eighty.

Moving in this body was hard. He wasn't used to the weight, the power. He tripped over his own feet and fell.

The rex was on him again, roaring and spitting in hunger and rage. Bertram hunkered down fast and beat his tail on the ground. The T. rex backed away.

Although Bertram had moved only a few feet, it was enough. Now he could see a wall of tangled vines, dense bushes, and very tall trees. Between the lower reaches of the thick high trees, roots and branches intertwined to form a terrible barrier. But at its center was a way out. Sunlight poured through a single, very low opening.

All Bertram had to do was get to the opening without getting eaten. If only there was some way he could distract the T. rex...

An idea flashed in his mind. Bertram concentrated on raising his tail straight up. The T. rex leaned forward. Then Bertram swayed his tail gently from one side to the other. The T. rex's head followed the movements perfectly.

Suddenly, Bertram rushed the T. rex, beating his tail on the ground and hollering defiantly! Startled, the predator leaped to one side.

Instantly, the T. rex roared and raced after its prey. Bertram hunkered down again and whipped his tail around. It smashed the remains of an old tree trunk, sending chunks of wood flying and distracting the T. rex once more.

Bertram lunged for the opening, but moving in this body was like scrambling on his hands and knees. He was slow compared to the blinding movements of the rex.

As Bertram's Ankylosaurus head brushed against the curtain of leaves at the near end of the corridor, he heard the rex's jaws snapping behind him. Quickly, Bertram pushed through the opening. The harsh sunlight on the other side blinded him, and the ground tilted violently. With a shrill cry, he was sliding down a sharp incline.

Trees lining the hill snapped as he struck them. His body banged against heavy rocks as he tumbled end over end, and he felt every bruising, jarring impact. Finally, he skidded toward the base of the incline. He flipped over one more time, onto his spiky back, his tail curled up and trapped under him. A cloud of dirt rose up as rocks and debris scattered down around him. Then it was over.

He'd landed belly-up.

Oh, no.

Bertram tried to move, but all he could do was make his front and rear paws wriggle in the air. An image came to mind: a sixteen-wheeler flipped onto its back, its wheels spinning helplessly.

Looks like I'm not going anywhere.

From somewhere above and behind him, the T. rex roared in frustration. Bertram knew he was vulnerable like this, with his belly completely exposed. He tried to free his trapped tail, but all he could do was make it twitch.

Looking down, he saw a small clearing at the base of the incline. It bordered another deep woods, filled with Araliopsoides, lush, leafy ginseng trees rising about thirty feet.

Suddenly, he smelled a powerful scent similar to the rank odor of the predator's breath. Heavy footfalls came his way. The ground shuddered. Thick tree branches snapped like twigs.

"No..." Bertram pleaded. "Please, no."

A shape appeared between two trees. Another T. rex! This one was emerald-and-rust-colored. But he looked just as big, fierce, and hungry as the last one.

"Please," Bertram whispered.

The T. rex lumbered closer. The claws at the end of his tiny arms were making strange little clicking noises. His maw hung open. He was *drooling*.

Unlike the other rex, he didn't roar. He just kept coming closer and closer, the sunlight glinting off his dagger-shaped six-inch-long teeth. Bertram had seen fossils of teeth like these. He knew that each inch-wide tooth was able to pierce meat and puncture bone. The Tyrannosaurus' jaw was powerful enough to tear off as much as five hundred pounds of flesh at one time!

"Please!" Bertram yelled. "Don't eat me! *Please!*"

The T. rex was close in now, opening his maw even wider. His teeth were inches from Bertram's exposed, quivering belly! Bertram shut his eyes.

"Pleeeeeeeeeeeeeeeeeeeeeeeeeeeeeeeeeeeeeeeeeeeeease!"

He waited. And waited. Finally, he heard another voice. "Bertram, is that *you* in there?"

Bertram's gaze locked on the rex's face. "Mike?"

The T. rex slowly nodded. Bertram's entire body sagged with relief. Tears formed in his eyes as he began to laugh.

He was no longer alone.

CHAPTER 2

MIKE

Mike stared down at the trapped club-tail.

Bertram looked so pitiful, wriggling there on his back, his belly exposed. Mike listened patiently as Bertram went on about his science fair project and some dinosaur bone he'd used.

"It was supposed to be for luck," Bertram said, shaking his enormous head. "But if my Memory INterpreter Device matched what it found in my subconscious with patterns from the molecular composition of that bone, well, that might explain why it sent us here."

"You mean you *wanted* to come here?" Mike asked.

Bertram snuffled. "I don't know. It's just a theory. Mr. London and I talk about that kind of stuff all the time. The collective unconscious. And the possibility of its extension to an organic memory. How the cycle of life on a molecular level stretches back to the origins of life in the universe. I mean—I didn't mean—I'm *scared*, Mike!"

29

Mike couldn't follow what Bertram was saying. He looked down at his tiny scale-covered arms and shook his head. It whipped back and forth so quickly he became dizzy and wanted to sit down. Only...he didn't know *how* to sit down as a T. rex.

This world was so strange.

The air was dense with insects. Mike didn't know if he could get used to the constant buzzing and humming. Bees landed on him. Bugs crawled all over him. Ants. Cockroaches. *Disgusting!*

Mike shuddered and stamped in place, trying to knock them off.

Suddenly, a nearby movement caught his attention. A pair of rabbit-sized hoofed animals moved closer. They looked part cat, part rat, and, well, part horse, tiny as they were. They crawled onto Bertram's belly and snatched away large leaves that were stuck to him. Then they kind of *galloped* away.

"Bertram?" Mike asked. "What was that?"

"A pair of Protoungulatums, I think. Forerunners of horses, antelopes, camels, and so on. Extinct now. Then. Later—" Bertram growled with frustration. "In our time."

"Oh."

Silence walled itself up between them for a moment. Then Bertram said, "What if there is no way back? What if we're stuck here forever? What if—?"

"Listen to me," Mike interrupted.

"What—?"

"*Listen to me*. You designed this machine, right?"

"Yeah, but not to do what—"

"Would you have made a machine that could only send us one way?"

"Wuh—uh—no—of course not."

"Then I believe there is a way back. There has to be. We just have to figure out what it is."

Mike felt a sudden rumbling inside him. A low growl came from his stomach. He was hungry. He took a step toward the writhing hot lunch before him and opened his gigantic razor-lined maw.

"*Mike!*" Bertram screamed.

Mike got ahold of himself. "Sorry. Instinct."

"Uh-huh. Right. No problem," said the Ankylosaurus, but he was visibly trembling.

Mike closed his eyes. He wondered if now would be a good time for a nervous breakdown. This was crazy. How could he buy into any of it?

An hour ago he'd been an athlete. The next Steve Young. That had been his dream. To one day measure up to his idol. His human body was a finely tuned machine that had never let him down. He wanted it back.

And yet...a part of him was *relieved* to be here instead of in his own time, in his own body. So long as he was here and not there, he didn't have to worry about the *big event* his buddy Sean had planned for today's practice. Mike had known about it for weeks— and he'd been sick over the whole thing just as long.

"Mike?" Bertram asked, sounding excited.

Mike opened his eyes. "Sorry. A lot on my mind."

"I think I've worked out how we're communicating. You're not really *hearing* anything when I talk. We're like...made of thought. Pure energy. We're just brainwaves. Somehow we can hear each other. It has something to do with the M.I.N.D. Machine. It linked us up."

"Okay..."

"We still move our mouths when we speak, but it's just habit. If we make any sound at all, it's just..." The Ankylosaurus made a clicking, grunting noise.

"Gotcha," Mike said.

Bertram suddenly waved his paws wildly. "Um, uh, Mike, listen. You think you could help me up? I mean, I can't stay like this. What if some other predator—"

"I'm *not* a predator," Mike said sharply.

Bertram trembled. "Mike, *please*."

Mike nodded. He had to stop thinking about Sean. Sean and his talk of how they all were *predators* and that without a killer instinct, not one single member of the team would survive.

"All right, let's get you loose." Mike reached out with his hands, forgetting they were now tiny two-fingered claws, and found he couldn't reach very far. He leaned forward, grasping with his claws, and banged heads with Bertram.

"Ow!" he cried, expecting a surge of pain in his skull. But all he felt was a dull thud.

"I didn't feel much of anything," Bertram said.

"Huh!" Mike said. "Me neither, really. Let's try it again."

"Um...okay."

Mike thrust his skull forward, colliding with Bertram's. There was a sharp crack.

"Cool!" said Mike. "It's like wearing a football helmet!"

Mike whonked his head against Bertram's and started laughing. "This is something!"

Bertram rolled his eyes. "I hate being stuck like this."

"Oh, right. Sure."

"Hmmmm," Bertram said, "I was thinking, how about using your feet to help free me? You've got those powerful legs. You can put your tail down and use it to balance. Try that."

Mike looked behind him and saw that he'd managed to keep his tail up at all times. Some things just came naturally.

Mike forced his tail down onto the ground, hoping to use it like a tripod, as Bertram had suggested. Then he balanced on one leg and dug his opposite foot into the pile of rocks surrounding Bertram.

The moment he tried to kick upward, Mike lost his balance. He tried to use his tail to compensate, but he moved it in the wrong direction. The world spun, and Mike fell backward. He landed with explosive impact, a cloud of dirt and rock flying up around him.

For a moment, Mike just lay there on his back. *Some athlete I am,* he thought. Then he tried bending at the waist to reach a sitting position. All he could do was yank himself partway up, as if he was trying to perform a sit-up, then flop back to the ground. A thunderclap of noise marked each attempt.

Mike rolled to his side and tried to push off that way, but his arms were too little to be much help. Finally, he lay back, panting. "I feel like such a loser."

"You're not a loser. If you were a loser, you'd have enough free time on your hands to memorize the names of every tree, shrub, and creepy-crawly thing in the Mesozoic."

"Bertram..."

"Forget it, Mike, just let me think. There has to be a way." Then Bertram said, "Try getting on your belly."

Mike did. He used his little arms to push up. Immediately, he flopped back down, unable to manage it.

"Okay," Bertram said. "Forget your arms. Get your legs up underneath you. Pretend it's track. You do track near the end of the year, right?"

"Sure. Football, baseball, track. I've got to keep myself in condition—"

"Pretend you're trying to get into the starting position. Only without your arms. Just your legs."

"Okay, I get it." Mike moved one leg, then the other. He managed to haul one foot under his belly, planting it firmly on the ground.

"There you go, you got it!" Bertram cried.

Mike pushed off and tried to get his other foot up in time. He swayed, slammed his tail down for balance—and lost it completely. Mike roared with frustration as he hit the ground.

"Chill," Bertram said. "It's going to take a few tries. Go on, give it another shot."

Mike tried it again. He almost had it, then he went down.

"Come on, Mike. *A winner never quits, and a quitter never wins*. You know that."

"Coach Garibaldi!"

"That's right."

"How do you know about that?"

"I've been to some games."

"Really? You?"

"Yeah, me. Even geeks like football."

Mike looked at Bertram. "I never called you that. I never even thought that. Don't put words in my mouth. Especially not words like *that*."

"Sorry," Bertram said. "I hate being helpless. I feel so stupid."

"You're *not* stupid. Just wait."

Mike tried four more times. On the fifth try, he managed to get to his feet. He tottered for a moment, then straightened himself out. *I did it!*

"All right!" Bertram cried. "Hey, tail off the ground!"

"Right. Thanks." Mike lifted his tail. "Now what?"

"Now flip me over!"

Mike's broad shoulders sagged. They were right back where they started. Then he saw a three-foot-long turtle with a golden shell, peppered with pockmarks, ambling toward the trees. It had a long neck and a pointy nose, and it gave Mike an idea.

"Wait a minute," Mike said. "One time my whole family was camping. We found this turtle flipped over on its back, just like you are. When we tried to grab its shell to help it, the turtle snapped and bit at us. It didn't understand we were trying to help."

"So what'd you do?"

Mike walked over to the fallen tree. He glanced back at Bertram. "How strong would you say I am?"

"Plenty strong. Your arms can lift over four hundred and fifty pounds."

"Good." Mike stomped at the branches on the ground, breaking them off. Then he wrapped his tiny arms around the log he'd made, and lifted it.

"Tell me you're not..." Bertram said.

Grunting, Mike shoved the log up against the club-tail's flank. "I weigh too much!" protested Bertram. "This won't work! I'll end up as a shish kebab!"

"An Ankylobob, you mean," Mike teased giddily as he worked the makeshift lever under Bertram's bulk.

"It's not going to work," Bertram repeated.

"Don't be such an Eeyore."

"Whaddya mean?"

"You know, in *Winnie-the-Pooh*. Eeyore. The donkey. The one who's always gloom and doom."

"The realist."

"Okay, that's it," Mike said with a laugh. "Now you're about to get a positive experience whether you like it or not!"

Mike dropped down onto the exposed end of the log. Incredibly, Bertram's right side was lifted up into the air by several feet.

"Whoa!" the Ankylosaurus hollered. The log began to crack. Mike had been expecting this. He shifted his weight and, avoiding Bertram's spikes, drove his shoulder into the hard shell of the Ankylosaurus. He pulled one foot up under him, then the other, and heaved with all his strength!

"*Miiiiiiiiiiiiiiiiiiiiiiike!*" Bertram yelled.

Bertram was now teetering on his side like a quarter that had fallen onto its edge. His legs shook and his tail whipped frantically.

Mike had to do something. What?

An idea came to him. He went down on his knees again, knowing full well that if his new plan failed, he'd never be able to get out of the way in time.

Picking up the log he'd used as a lever, Mike thrust it like a spear at Bertram's shell. It connected just as the club-tail's body sank back toward Mike.

"Oh, no," Mike whispered. He stood up, putting all the power he had left into one final push—

A moment later, Bertram flopped over, onto his

belly! He landed with a yelp of surprise.

Mike's tiny arms flew into the air. He whooped as he hopped from one foot to the other, slapping his tail in a victory dance. "Ooooh, yeah! All right! Can't touch me tonight! Nuh-uh!"

Bertram watched happily until Mike's stomach growled again. "Okay, what do we do about *this?*" asked Mike. "T. rexes are meat-eaters, right? I mean— a part of me wants to eat *you!*"

Bertram took a half step back.

"You know I won't," Mike assured his friend. "It's just—I'm not eating the locals. I don't care *what* this body wants. I'd rather starve. Really."

Mike looked at all the greens surrounding him. "Hey, I can just go vegetarian, right? Have a salad."

Bertram shook his head. "Your body won't run on vegetable matter. It can't digest it. That's why there are carnivores, who eat meat, and herbivores, who eat plants."

"So, what do we do?"

Bertram appeared lost in thought. Then his eyes lit up. "You and your family ever go fishing?"

"Um...sure."

"Then that's what we'll do. First, we have to find salt water. In the Cretaceous period, an inland sea divided the land that would become the United States. My new nose is pretty good, and I smell something that makes me think we're near the shore. But you're a lot higher off the ground. You should be able to find an exact direction. Your nose knows."

"My nose knows?"

"Your nose knows. Trust me."

Mike gave Bertram a strange look. *Your nose knows.* What did Bertram mean by that? Mike took a deep breath—and found out.

"Whoa!" Mike cried. So many strange scents—information overload! His chest heaved and his body trembled as he tried to make sense of all the smells.

"Trust your instincts, Mike. It's just like you're playing football. Relax and go with your gut."

Mike's new Tyrannosaurus gut was the last thing he wanted to trust. But he was hungry, and a rough, growling, animal part of his brain was ready to separate all of those scents he'd just experienced into two essential categories: food and non-food. Bertram fell into the first category.

"Sea water...it's salty. Smelly. Think about that," said Bertram. "Try to concentrate on that."

"Okay," Mike said. He took another breath, not quite so deep this time. He pictured the beach, the tang of sea water, then he pointed with his short little arms. "The water's that direction. It's a ways off, but I can smell it."

Mike's stomach growled. It was a low, deep, reverberating sound.

"We better get going," Bertram said.

Mike sniffed again. "That's weird. I'm smelling... don't laugh—"

"Tell me."

"I'm smelling *fear*. Something really terrified. Coming this way."

Bertram nodded.

"And it's not alone. Whatever's scaring it is coming toward us, too." Mike sniffed one more time. "Bertram, the *whatever* that's scaring it?"

"Uh-huh..."

"There's a lot of *whatevers* on the way."

CHAPTER 3

CANDAYCE

Help meeeeeeeeeeeeeeeeeeeeeeeeeeeeee!

Candayce Chambers plunged through the dense, buzzing, insect-infested woods, monsters at her heels.

Things that might have been roaches or rats scurried at her feet, but she didn't look down. She had a sense that other *things* were watching her from the trees, but she couldn't concern herself with them right now. Her pursuers were dinosaurs. T. rexes. Just like in the movies. Except—and this would have been the funny part if she'd been in a mood to laugh instead of scream—they were just little guys. Pint-sized!

Ha-ha. Big funny. They were trying to kill her!

All right, Candayce, she commanded herself, *you're going to wake up. Now!*

She didn't. So she ran. Branches snapped against her body, but she felt no pain, only a weird bloatedness. Ahead, she saw flashes of brown and green and amber. Tangled roots and soft blue-white daggers of sunlight. She sniffed. The whole area smelled bad. As

41

if a thousand dogs had just been walked and there wasn't a pooper-scooper to be found.

Her legs moved awkwardly as she continued her flight. They were strong and powerful, but thick and squat, like stumpy tree trunks, if that made any sense. Of course, this was just a dream, and dreams didn't have to make sense.

She looked over her shoulder at the rexes heading her way. They were green-and-gray, their scales spotted and striped with dull purples and yellows. Their maws hung open, revealing rows of razor-sharp teeth. Saliva sprayed in every direction. The monsters grunted and growled like football players chasing cheerleaders after a winning game. Disgusting!

She ran faster than she ever had before, but it wasn't enough. She'd managed to outdistance her pursuers so far by going low and ducking through tangled networks of underbrush where they couldn't follow. But they always caught up.

She burst into a wide-open area at the foot of a large drop-off. Another pair of monsters rose up in front of her. One was short and squat, covered in spikes. It looked a little like a turtle, only it was about thirty times the size of any turtle she'd ever seen. The other was a giant T. rex. It was easily *twice* the size of the creatures closing in behind her.

She was trapped! No, she wouldn't accept that. Her sensei's words came to her: *Always do the unexpected. Zig when your opponent expects you to zag.*

Under normal circumstances, Candayce wouldn't pay a lot of attention to the life lessons her sensei imparted. To her, martial arts was just exercise. It was trendy, it was fun, and it let her get some of her anger out.

But these were hardly normal circumstances, so this time she listened. Tearing *between* the T. rex and the big spiked turtle thingee, Candayce was past the monsters and at the bottom of the incline in seconds. She'd been hiking mountains half her life, and she wagered the dinosaurs chasing her wouldn't be any good at it.

"Candayce! Stop, wait!" the club-tail yelled.

She froze. It was a dream, so *of course* the big spiky turtle-looking guy would know her name. Why question it?

She resumed running, thinking about her therapist. Her therapist got a hundred dollars an hour, and his duties included helping her dispel bad dreams. He'd given her techniques for guiding the course of her night visions—staying in control of them.

None of the tricks she'd learned were working. The nightmarish scene remained in place.

"Candayce!" another voice. *Mike's voice*. It had come from the T. rex. She looked back despite herself.

Over her shoulder, she saw Mike—no, that couldn't be right, not even in a dream, it was just too weird—confront the half-sized rexes. He let out a roar that made her place her hands over her ears.

Weird how clammy her skin felt. Yet dried-out. What she wouldn't do for some moisturizer. In fact, all of her skin felt hard and callused. And what was that weird *weight* she felt on her behind?

Something told her not to look, but she did.

A long pastel-colored tail stuck out between her hips. It was attached to a reptilian-looking spine. Both were mustard yellow with pimento red toppings: stripes on the tail, spots on her back.

She looked down at her thighs and nearly gagged. What had happened to her? Her thighs were *enormous!* And she had a pot belly! And her chest was *flat*. Not to mention scaly. She had wrinkles and rings and

lines and dents! And she was naked!

An instant before her mind could give out totally, an idea came to her: Someone had dressed her in a weird costume for this dream, that's all it was.

Well, she didn't like it one bit!

A chorus of growls dragged her attention away from what was *usually* her favorite topic—herself. And for once, she was glad.

She saw that forty feet away, Mike was kicking rocks at the smaller rexes, scattering them. The spiky turtle guy was attacking, too! He swung his club-tail, and a couple of the little guys went flying!

Mike roared and slammed his tail onto the ground. The earth beneath Candayce shuddered. She heard a sliding sound from above and turned as rocks trickled down from the incline. He'd started an avalanche!

"Yow!" Candayce hollered as the rocks hit her head. Weird how the stones felt so light. They hardly hurt at all when they connected. The "avalanche" ended quickly. She studied the incline. No way could she get a decent foothold. Looking back again, she saw the smaller rexes fleeing.

The big one turned toward her. Candayce was paralyzed by his gaze. She wondered if the only reason he'd fought off the other creatures was so that he could have her for himself. For breakfast.

You're not going to faint, she told herself, even though her head was feeling light. *You're not going to do anything that—that—girly...Do you hear me?*

Girly? she immediately chided herself. *If Mike Tyson was looking at that, he'd be laid out, too!*

The giant T. rex took a step her way. "Candayce, it's me. It's Mike. You don't have to be afraid."

This was too funky. Too much for anyone to expect her to be able to handle. Why couldn't she wake herself up from this bizarro dream? The T. rex came a little closer. The ground shuddered with his approach.

Candayce suddenly became aware of two very different sets of instincts within her. One set of instincts told her to trust Mike. He was always a nice guy. Too nice for his own good half the time.

The other set of instincts told her to run like the wind and not look back.

One set of instincts was hers. The other wasn't.

Candayce stood still. "Mike?"

"It's me. The guy with the tail is Bertram."

"But you're dinosaurs."

"Yeah. It's going around."

Candayce wondered what he meant. Then she looked over her shoulder and down at her tail once more. The tail was twitching. *She* was making it twitch.

"Oh, no," she whispered. "No, no, no..."

Candayce held her hands up to her face. They weren't hands. They were scaly paws. Or claws. Kind of. Three sharp fingers and two other stubby things that formed a, well, a *hoof*. Like a horse might have.

She tried touching her face. The hardened scales

were there, too. She had a ridge over her forehead. Like an upturned collar. Her jaws were like a set of pliers, only sharp at the tip. She had some kind of beak or something. Her lips were gone. Her hair was gone. Her pert, petite little nose was gone.

Her head felt light again. She sank down and landed on all fours. That *other* set of instincts inside her told her this was a natural position.

"Oh," she said. Followed by an "I," then a "What?" followed by a handful of words she never used when other people were around, ending with a strangled, tear-filled cry.

"I'm ugly and I'm naked and I'm covered with bugs. There are bugs crawling all over me!"

"I know. It's annoying."

"Annoying? Annoying doesn't begin to cover it! What am I, some kind of *animal?*"

"Actually—" Bertram began.

"Shut up! Just shut up!" Candayce wailed. She fell back and squatted, trying her best to cover her chest. "I'm a monster."

"Actually," said the club-tail as he came forward, "you're a Leptoceratops. A crested dinosaur. Distinguished by the parrotlike beak and the Triceratops-like body construction."

"No, no, no," Candayce repeated. "This is a dream, and I'm going to wake up."

"It's not," Mike said. "It's not a dream. I'm sorry. We're...we're stuck here. At least until we can figure out a way back. It's a long story."

"No, no, no," Candayce continued.

In reply, the spiky turtlelike club-tailed meandering know-it-all dinosaur thingee said, "Just in case you were wondering, those dinos who were chasing you were Nanotyrannus. Pygmy dinosaurs. There's speculation as to whether they're just young T. rexes or a separate genus. *Controversy,* actually, but with paleontology, that kind of thing happens."

"No, no, no," Candayce said once more. She suddenly felt as if her mind were lost in a whirlwind.

"Help! Help! I can't fly! Help!" The sharp, piercing cry came from above. Candayce didn't look up. She knew that voice. It was *Janine*.

Suddenly, Candayce realized she was trapped. In the past. In the body of a gross little dinosaur. With Mike. And some geek. And Janine, the Wicked Witch of the Eastern Flats.

"No, no, no," Candayce chanted again. She wanted to run. Only her body wouldn't move. Her eyes just went kind of glassy.

No, no, no, she thought.

Then she didn't think anything else.

And she was happy.

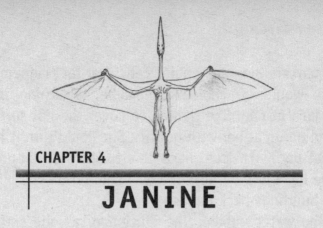

CHAPTER 4

JANINE

Janine Farehouse could see her reflection in the waters below. She knew what she had become. And she knew she wasn't dreaming.

She was a Pterodactyl. Her wings were dark crimson and Day-Glo blue, and they stretched fifteen feet from tip to tip. She had claws—but no teeth.

And she was flying. Or so she'd told herself, until she realized that she had confused *flying* with *falling*. She was descending rapidly—at high speed. The world was flashing past in a blur.

She screamed!

She flapped her wings, and the world flipped over a half-dozen times. She plunged straight down like a weight tossed out of a 747. The water reached up for her, glassy and smooth. Hard as diamond. She could see her own reflection—or actually the reflection of the sleek, magnificent flyer in which she was now residing. It was like falling into a mirror.

A crazy thought came to her. She wished she had

her markers, her spray paint cans. Her fat Magnum 44 black would be choice. Or maybe something in a German Fat Cap. She wanted to cover the flat surface barreling up at her with graffiti. She could turn it into a real burner, a true piece of art. She'd be proud to leave her tag here, just the way she did on the buses and buildings back home.

The water rippled. The illusion of a solid surface melted and vanished as two huge emerald-and-onyx bumps rose up. Then a twenty-six-foot-long neck unfurled, writhing like a snake. The head at the end of the neck snapped its mass of shining, needlelike teeth at the precise spot where Janine would soon plunge.

Janine freaked. She wriggled her long arms, and by extension her wings. She tried to flap, tried to sail, tried to soar, but she couldn't halt this terrible descent. The creature below snapped its maw and ground its teeth together in anticipation.

Without warning, Janine went cold. Her emotions turned off. Her fear cut out. She studied the situation calmly, determined to think of something.

This sort of thing had happened to her only twice before in her thirteen years. Once, when news came that her father had been killed overseas and she had to be strong to hold her mom together. And another time, when she and her older cousin were on the Hi-Line, good old Highway 2, and a blowout sent them careening toward a Montana double-date—two guys and two dogs sitting in the cab of a midnight black pickup truck. Without a single tremor of fear, she'd analyzed the situation, seized the wheel from Margie, and saved their lives.

It was time to grab the wheel again. She looked calmly at what was happening: She was in the body of a Pterodactyl, and she was falling to her death. It was a safe bet that this body still held a prior occupant. If so, it was the only chance they both had now.

Janine searched inside. A consciousness rose up, the buried mind of the Pterodactyl. The Pterodactyl inside her sensed a current of air ten feet over the snapping head of the sea creature. The flyer spread her wings and angled herself into the draft.

This is going to work! Janine told herself.

There was a sound like a massive sheet being whipped by the wind—

Thhhhhhhhhhhhhwwwwwwwacccccccccccck!

Then came a yanking and the rustle of wings, and Janine was being lifted up and away from the danger! She heard the angry cry of the sea creature and an incredible splash below. Then she saw a mighty shape burst from the water—but she didn't care. She was sailing away, the wind catching hold of her hollow bones.

The momentum she'd gained from the sudden nosedive robbed her of the chance to ascend. All she could do was glide to a landing, skipping along the frothy water until she came to rest on the surface.

She spun in a slow circle, relief flooding through

her. Then, slowly, a nightmare came into view: The sea creature was only a hundred feet away. Its head and neck were raised, its rounded back arched in a hump. Flippers in the front and rear slapped at the water.

Janine had seen this particular monster before. Or something just like it. Images from grainy old photographs entered her mind.

Nessie. *The Loch Ness Monster.* A prehistoric creature where Janine came from. A not-so-friendly native here and now.

Janine dimly recalled reading a book about a pair of children who had wondrous encounters with Nessie. Somehow, that book had left out a lot about the Elasmosaurus' predatory nature.

Janine's calm vanished. So did the mind of the Pterodactyl. Logic told her that if there was any way out of this, the Pterodactyl would have at least dropped a clue before it split.

It hadn't. She was fish food.

Suddenly, a shadow fell upon her. Janine looked up and saw another Pterodactyl whipping over her, flying straight for the sea monster's head!

The newcomer was golden with streaks of gray, blue, and scarlet. He loosed an ear-piercing scream and soared to the right and then to the left.

Nessie was fascinated. The creature watched the new Pterodactyl sail past, spin, then perform a perfect figure eight. Nessie snapped furiously, but the tricky newcomer always remained out of reach.

"Janine, swim for it!" someone called. She recognized the voice. She was about to reply, "Bertram?" when it occurred to her that it didn't matter who was delivering the advice—she'd better just take it!

Paddling, she turned and looked toward shore. She could see a T. rex and an Ankylosaurus trying to get her attention.

She didn't know much about paleontology—not like Bertram—but she knew enough to recognize that the rex and the club-tail were natural enemies, stemming from very different branches on the tree of life. Yet there they were, standing side by side as if it were the most natural thing in the world.

A roar sounded behind her. She craned her neck and looked back to see her tricky Pterodactyl friend dive right into the Elasmosaurus' reach, then dart away at the last second.

Nessie looked frustrated. She wanted prey she could actually capture. She wanted *Janine*.

Janine paddled and kicked, nearly submerging herself twice. She heard the sighs of the waves turn to hisses and roars as they rose and fell behind her. She could *feel* the Elasmosaurus closing in.

Suddenly, a pair of fins cut through the water beneath her raised wing. A dark gray shape glided beside her. Janine froze as the waves revealed an Ischyrhizz, a seven-foot-long saw shark.

Oh, good, she told herself, *a killing machine with a Ginsu knife attachment.*

The shark dove beneath the water. Janine relaxed, but only a little. The waves were driving her to shore. She looked back and saw the other Pterodactyl, whom she now thought of as the Trickster, diving in close enough to scrape at Nessie with the tip of his wing.

Enraged, the Elasmosaurus forgot about Janine and went back to snapping at the Trickster. She nearly snagged him with her first try, and Janine feared for her mysterious savior.

"Over here!" she hollered at Nessie. "You stupid old, stupid..."

She couldn't come up with an insult. Not for a fish. People—fine, no problem. But trying to diss a fish was beyond her.

It didn't matter. Nessie heard her insults. Or she heard *something*, anyway. Janine understood that huma sounds were no longer coming out of her. Instead, she was making the same piercing cries as the other Pterodactyl.

Nessie turned toward Janine. Another great tidal

wave rushed up, carrying Janine a dozen feet into the air. Like a surfer, she was hurled over the water for an instant, then slapped down and nearly tugged under.

A pair of five-foot-long sharks sailed beneath her, apparently fed and uninterested. Thank goodness.

Slow-moving, four- to six-inch-long invertebrates in mother-of-pearl shells swam by, their cilia flickering. The sun bounced off their iridescent shells, creating a rainbow of color. Eight-inch-long lobsterlike Linuparus with spiny armored bodies drifted near. A school of blue-colored fish sped around her. Their jaws were filled with curved and interlocked elongated teeth. They attacked smaller jelly-bodied fish.

Janine kept swimming hard and fast, watching the sand beneath the water rising higher and higher...

Finally, she looked back and saw the Elasmosaurus stuck several yards back in the deep. She wanted to laugh and cry in triumph! She'd made it. She was safe!

Then Nessie's great neck extended, all two dozen feet of it, and the head came down at Janine.

Janine screamed! And the T. rex let out the most frightening roar Janine had ever heard. Nessie froze.

"Now!" Bertram's voice cried. "The shore!"

Using her wings as paddles, Janine covered the last few feet separating her from the beach. Trembling, she walked onto shore with her spindly but strong rear legs, then folded her wings around her like a cloak.

Shells of every description littered the shore, painting it in stunning colors. Funnel-like shells, clam-shaped, teardrop-shaped, and a few that looked like small round castles, all mixed together with wreaths of coral. Her feet crunched as she walked. Tiny hermit crabs scampered nearby. Mollusks, limpets, snails, and a few of the lobsters were scattered about.

She turned back to look at Nessie, who railed in frustration, snapped her jaws at the other pterosaur, then slipped back beneath the waves.

"Are you okay?" Bertram asked.

Janine faced the club-tail and his T. rex companion. For the first time, she noticed that another dinosaur lay at their feet. It was an ugly, squat, garishly colored little thing with a parrotlike face and a nasty set of thunder thighs. Its eyes were glassy, and it drooled a little.

"Yeah," Janine said. "I'm okay."

Above, a great sharp *caw* sounded. Janine looked up to see her new friend circling overhead. The Trickster looked down at her, then regarded her companions with a look that Janine somehow felt was one of disdain. With a snort, he flew off, dive-bombing the Elasmosaurus one last time for good measure.

Janine looked nervously at the T. rex, then back to Bertram. "Friend of yours?"

The Ankylosaurus angled his head in the T. rex's direction. "Mike Peterefsky. Yeah, he's friendly enough—for a predator."

"I'm not a predator," Mike said with a weak sigh.

Then he looked with concern toward the small lumpy yellow-and-red dinosaur at his feet.

"I hope I wasn't too rough," the T. rex began. "I had to carry her in my claws, y'know, by the leg, upside down, the whole way. I didn't know how else to get her to come with us. I couldn't leave her."

"You should have seen it," Bertram said. "Mike dragged *me* the whole way by putting my tail in his mouth. He chipped a bunch of teeth doing it, but—"

"We're dinosaurs," Janine said.

"Yep," replied Bertram.

Janine gestured to the glassy-eyed Leptoceratops. "Who's Thunder-Thighs?"

"Candayce Chambers," Mike said.

Janine's head sunk to her chest. The rustle of wings surprised her, but only a little. She was already getting used to this. "What happened to her?"

Mike threw his little T. rex hands into the air. "She just...checked out. I'll carry her. It's no problem."

Janine looked back to the horizon, where the Trickster was heading. "So who's he?"

"What do you mean?" Mike asked.

Janine gestured in the other Pterodactyl's direction. "Which lucky eighth grader is that?"

Bertram cleared his throat. "I believe he's indigenous."

Janine was surprised. Her savior was the real thing. An actual Pterodactyl. "Smart sucker. Tricky."

She looked back at the Elasmosaurus kicking

around in the waves. Then she saw its head dip beneath the water and come up with a wriggling four-foot-long shark. It turned, and swam off.

"Yeah," she said. "So will someone *please* tell me what we're doing here, why we can understand each other when we're not really talking out loud, and what we have to do to get home?"

The T. rex and the club-tail were silent for a moment. Bertram spoke first. "We're working on that."

Suddenly, a crackling sound made everyone jump. Janine looked up, expecting to see lightning streaking across the sky. But there was nothing. No, that wasn't true. She heard a low, deep humming, and it was accompanied by a tingling at the back of her skull.

"Guys? Do you feel—"

Before she could finish, a second crackling and the sense of some alien force rippled through the air all around them. It was electric. Terrifying!

A voice rose out of the crackling.

Bertram! Bertram, can you hear me? I pray that you can. This is Mr. London. I know what's happened—and I think I can help...

CHAPTER 5

BERTRAM

Mr. London's words energized Bertram. "I can hear you!" There was no reply. "Mr. London, I can—"
The crackling came again.

I don't have much time. I don't know if this will work. It's a one-way transmission, so don't bother trying to respond. Just listen.

Bertram fell silent, the gazes of the others upon him. As usual, Janine's seemed to penetrate his soul. The voice went on.

Bertram, what I'm about to say may sound odd, even confusing at first, but hear me out. If my calculations are correct, then for you, the accident that sent you and the others into the past has just happened. But for me, it

*occurred over sixty years ago. I'm not the Mr.
London you once knew. I'm a very old man. I'm
from what you would think of as the future.
One possible future, anyway.*

*In my reality, after the lightning struck,
you and the others collapsed and appeared to
be in comas. For the past sixty years of my
time, you've remained that way.*

"No," Bertram whispered. He looked at Mike,
Janine, and Candayce. They appeared equally shocked.
"You can't just tell us that," Mike hollered.
"There's no hope," Janine whispered.
"Stop it!" Bertram cried. Mr. London was still talk-
ing, and he was missing things that were being said.

*I've spent my whole life trying to under-
stand what caused your M.I.N.D. Machine to
evolve and transform into a vessel capable of
extracting the true essence of a human being
from his or her body and sending it elsewhere
in time to live in the physical form of another.
From the machine's records, I know that's
what happened. Even so, the closest explana-
tion I can come up with is the theory of the
twelve monkeys.*

The twelve monkeys. He knew precisely what his
teacher meant, but this was no time to dwell on it.

The most important thing for you to understand is that my time is not the only time. My
reality is not the only reality. According to the
M.I.N.D. Machine, no transmission from the
past, present, or any possible future ever
reached you in the Late Cretaceous. That
means if you are hearing this message, the
past has already been changed. Your course
has been altered. It's proof positive that the
last sixty years I've lived can be undone. Now
it's up to you.

Bertram, for you to get back home, you
must find the Standing Stones, and you must
do it quickly. You don't have much time. If my
estimates are correct, you have about ten to
twelve days and a great deal of ground to
cover. Along with this message, I'm download-
ing a map that may help you.

Bertram could feel something entering his mind.

As to how accurate this map is, I cannot
say. All I can do is wish you luck and say that
I believe you can do this. Try, Bertram. For all
of us, try and change the past.

There's one more thing I have to tell you,
something you must know, or else you may not
make it back! Remember—

The transmission suddenly stopped. The teenagers stared at one another. They waited for the transmission to continue, for a second message to arrive.

The silence deepened.

"I think that's it," Janine said.

"Wait!" Bertram cried. "I know Mr. London. He wouldn't leave us hanging like that."

They waited. The silence became monstrous.

"Comas," Bertram whispered. "We end up spending our whole lives in comas." He looked around frantically. "My dad can't manage on his own, he—"

"That's only if we don't make it back," Mike said firmly. "We will. Don't doubt that for a *second*."

Mike sounded so confident. Bertram wanted badly to believe him.

Then Mike looked away and hung his wide head. "Course, if we don't..." He shuddered. "My dad—my dad'll be okay. He'll just keep going, put all his energy into the business. Construction business, y'know? Peterefsky Builders. But my mom. And Lee. My older brother, Lee, will probably have to come home from college. Probably *has*. I mean, it's already happened, right? We've already failed—"

"Stop it!" Bertram said, terrified. "Please."

Mike looked up. "Sorry. Guess I lost it there."

Janine opened her wings. "I don't want to think about this, I don't want to talk about this. It doesn't do us any good. We know what's at stake. What we have to figure out is what's our first move."

A loud rumbling slowly erupted from Mike's belly. Janine and Bertram looked his way. The sound came again. Even louder this time. Janine started to laugh.

"Stop it, we have to be quiet!" Bertram snapped.

"Tell *him* that." Janine broke into a loud guffaw as Mike's stomach again made its presence known.

Mike looked away. "This is so embarrassing..."

"You're embarrassed?" Janine asked. "At least you're a T. rex. I'm a flying reptile who doesn't know how to fly. A Pterodactyl who can't—"

"Actually," Bertram said, "you're a Quetzalcoatlus. Fairly young, I'd say. Your wingspan full-grown would be about thirty-six feet. You're the most perfect of the pterosaurs. The pinnacle of evolution. And as far as flying is concerned, you should try to get used to gliding first."

"Oh." Janine blinked. "Oh, okay. The *pinnacle,* huh?"

"Yes."

She nodded toward Candayce. "And what's she?"

"A Leptoceratops. Fairly common."

"Really? Hmm. This might not be so bad after all."

Bertram looked around. "There isn't any more to the message? That's all Mr. London could transmit?"

"My guess is for now, yeah," Janine said.

Bertram was silent for a long time, taking that in.

"What did he mean about the twelve monkeys?" Janine asked.

Bertram blinked. "There's an old saying. If you put

twelve monkeys in a room with twelve typewriters for a thousand years, eventually one of them will write *Hamlet*. It's about random chance. I think what Mr. London was getting at was that if I'd tried to build a machine that could do what the M.I.N.D. Machine did, the odds would have been a trillion to one against it. But somehow, without even trying, I put together all the right parts, in all the right ways. Just by pure random chance. Still, I can't help but think that there's more to it than that. In fact—"

"Listen," Mike said sharply. "Coach Garibaldi has a saying: 'What is, is. Deal with it.'"

"That's progressive," Janine muttered.

Bertram bobbed his head. "Actually, it is."

Mike's stomach growled again. He turned away and slapped his tail on the shore.

The impact made Janine stumble from her feet and land on her back.

"Oh, no, not this again," Bertram muttered, recalling his own painful attempts at righting himself.

Janine popped back up without hesitation.

"That's amazing!" Bertram exclaimed. "How'd you do that?"

Janine looked at him strangely. At least, it seemed strange to him. "I just...stood up. It's no big whup."

"You must have established a much greater rapport with the resident mind in your host body than either Mike or myself. You can help us—"

"Bertram," Janine said.

"Um...yeah?" asked the excited club-tail.

"I stood up. That's it. Let's not throw a parade over it, okay? We've got bigger issues to deal with."

"Right, right, right," Bertram said.

Mike's stomach went again. He shuffled a few yards from the others. "Oh, man!"

"Okay," Janine said in a take-charge tone, "we need to get him fed so he doesn't go native and start picturing us wrapped in hot-dog buns—"

"Hey!" Mike said.

"No offense," Janine added. "But my host is pretty passive. I have the feeling yours isn't."

Mike's head sunk low. "Yeah."

"She's right," Bertram said. "Our bodies are like massive engines. They require fuel."

Janine nodded. "I could go for a little something, too. Nearly dying and everything was kind of exhausting." She laughed. "Once we get some grub, or maybe on the way, we can talk about all this. I'm assuming you've got some idea what direction we need to go to reach the Standing Stones."

"Yeah," Bertram said. "In fact—"

Suddenly, a lower, basslike growling sounded. Bertram almost dismissed the sound, assuming it was coming from Mike. Then he looked over at Candayce, who was staring out at the waves.

Janine looked sharply in her direction. So did Mike.

Candayce's beak was opening and closing wordlessly. A tear was forming in the corner of her eye.

Images of food registered in Bertram's mind. He could *see* a plate full of mashed potatoes. He could *smell* the rich aroma of sautéed mushrooms and onions spread over a filet mignon. *Taste* the sweet perfection of a watermelon-ice drink...

Snap out of it! he chided himself. He dismissed the images. Mike and Janine's mouths were watering. Their eyes appeared a little vacant.

"Guys?" Bertram squeaked.

Janine looked over dreamily. Mike's upper lip curled back, showing his shiny teeth. He stared at Candayce as if she were the meal that had apparently just been projected into all of their minds.

"Guys!" Bertram hollered.

Mike started, then drew back in alarm. "Oh, *man...*"

Janine looked over. "Hot-dog buns?"

Mike nodded, and Janine tapped Mike's back with one wing. "Look, Mike and I are the meat-eaters. You and Candy Cane are the plant-eaters, right?"

Bertram nodded. Janine's ability to read her host's mind was astounding. That—or she had read up on paleontology. Either way, she was dead on.

"Fine," Janine said. "You take Sleeping Beauty into the woods, get her to eat some greens. Mike and I will stay here and do some fishing."

"Okay," Bertram said. He was edgy, still waiting, still *praying* that more of Mr. London's message would arrive. But somehow Janine's calm attitude was becoming infectious. "Come on, Candayce. There's a nice garden salad waiting for us this way."

He took a few slow steps toward the trees in the distance. Candayce's head wobbled in his direction.

"Do they serve Caesar? I like Caesar salads," Candayce murmured hazily.

"You bet," Bertram said. "Come on."

"Okey-doke." Candayce rose unsteadily and followed Bertram. He took one look back at Mike and Janine, then walked with Candayce into the woods.

It occurred to Bertram that this was kind of like a date. He'd known Candayce all his life, but this was the first time he'd really been alone with her. Though the circumstances couldn't have been any more bizarre, he was looking forward to the experience.

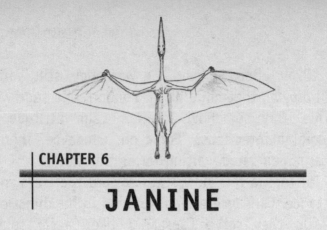

CHAPTER 6

JANINE

The sun torched the horizon as Janine walked toward the water with Mike beside her. When a birdlike cry rang out, she looked up, wondering if the Trickster had returned. Instead, from far down the beach, a pair of purple ducks waddled toward her and Mike.

"They're *huge*," Mike said.

Janine nodded. "I think they're called Hesperornis." The purple ducks were over five feet long. They had sharp teeth in their beaks. Mike growled at them, and they changed direction. They moved into the water, swam out, and dove as if rocket-propelled. Moments later, they emerged with mouthfuls of fish. Then a gray blur with teeth exploded from the water, snatched them up, and hauled them under.

"There's probably some smart remark I could make here," Janine said.

"Duck?" Mike offered feebly, lowering his head.

"Right." Janine glanced back at the trees. "Do you

think Bertram and Candayce will be okay?"

"Oh, sure. If they run into anything, all they have to do is yell. We'll hear 'em. I'm fast. To be honest, I can't believe how fast I can go in this." He gestured down at his bulk. "And Bertram's got that tail. He could use some practice swinging it."

Janine laughed. They waded into the water. "Keep an eye out, okay? I saw sharks before."

"All right," Mike said.

A strong wind rushed over the waves. Janine looked down, and a rainbow of color flashed beneath her. She poked her beak into the waters.

"Ow!" she hollered as her beak struck a rock. The impact reached all the way back to her skull.

When she looked back, the fish were gone.

"Sorry," Janine said. "I'm not used to judging distances too well."

"It's okay," Mike said. "We're all gonna need some practice sessions before we make this team."

Janine felt a sudden unease but didn't know why. It wasn't because of being in this strange new body. She was adjusting to that. So what was it?

She looked over at Mike and saw something in his eyes that told her exactly where this feeling had come from. She was getting a sense of his emotions. It was actually pretty overwhelming.

"Do you want to talk about it?" Janine asked.

Mike looked startled. "What?"

"Something's bothering you. I can tell."

Mike's claws went up. "It's this whole thing..."

"No. There's something *else*. I noticed it before the accident. When you were with Bertram, Candayce—"

"Really, there's—"

"—and Sean."

Mike turned away. Janine felt a hostile flare of emotion stab at her from her companion.

"It's nothing," Mike said.

"Oh." Janine had a sense that she had gotten to the root of the problem when she mentioned Sean. Everyone knew that Mike and Sean O'Malley weren't as close as they used to be. But no one seemed to know why. Janine decided not to push it.

Suddenly, Janine saw a silver-blue shark coming her way. She shrieked and darted back from the water.

Mike opened his maw and plunged his head into the cool shallows. There was an explosion of froth. Janine's vision blurred. She couldn't see what was happening as she raced back to the shore. Then she saw Mike staring quizzically at the waters.

"I think it's unconscious," Mike said. "I head-butted it. Now it keeps knocking into things. Wait a minute, okay, now it's going away. You can come back now. It's safe."

"Oh," Janine said. She stepped into the waters again, scrutinizing the shallows as she progressed.

"Janine, Janine—there, look!"

She saw it. Four little blue-colored fish. Her beak

darted into the water. It opened, taking in the bitter tang of salt water, then it closed swiftly, like a steel trap. "I don't think I—"

A sudden, disturbing sensation came to her. Something was swimming around in her mouth!

"Blllllawaaaaaaaaaaaaaaaa!" she screamed, opening her maw and shaking her beak frantically. She couldn't keep herself from swallowing.

"Oh, no," Janine whispered. "I swallowed them. I don't have any teeth, I guess that's what I'm supposed to do, but...this is so *gross*. I can feel them sliding down my throat!"

Mike's tiny arms drew up against his body, his shoulder went up, and he nodded a little too swiftly for the gesture to be casual. "Yeah, I can see them— little bumps going down your neck."

"Oh! Ah! Jeez! Yuck!" Trembling, she turned away. Then she felt movement in her gullet, slower, slower still, and finally, just a slight relief from the hunger pangs she'd been feeling. She faced Mike again.

"Are you okay?" he asked.

"You're gonna think this is disgusting," she said.

"Try me."

"It's really not that bad."

"Okay," he said as he looked down at the water again. His stomach growled.

"You really have to eat something, Mike. You do."

Looking amazingly timid for a T. rex, he bent low and studied the water. He took a few loud sniffs. Then he went a little farther out. Something about that disturbed Janine. She wasn't sure what, exactly. Just something. She said, "Stay close to shore."

"They're coming! A whole school. Dozens."

"Just be careful." She wondered what danger she'd sensed.

"This is no worse than going to a lobster bar," he muttered.

"What?" she asked.

His little hands gestured helplessly. "You know. Fresh fish. Seeing the little guys looking at you. With their tiny eyes and stuff." He hesitated. "I don't want to do this."

"You've never been fishing?"

He shook his head. "I told Bertram I had. I don't know why. I guess I didn't want to look—I dunno, like I couldn't handle it."

"Bertram would never judge you. You've seen the way he looks up to you."

Janine's words seemed to trigger that same strange unease in Mike once more. Weird. Sean, okay, Mike clearly had problems to work out with him, but why should talking about Bertram get Mike upset?

"Whatever," Mike said quickly.

Janine decided that she had to do something. It was funny. Mike Peterefsky didn't even know she was alive back in the real world. But here, it was as if they were suddenly best friends or something.

Mike sniffed again, then drove his head into the

water. Orange-and-red fish flew as his maw flashed and his teeth glistened. This time, Janine darted back before the impact of the waves could knock her down.

Terrible chomping sounds followed as Mike lifted his head. He took another step, drove his massive skull downward again, and roared with delight.

She waited on the shore until he was done. He came stomping up to her.

"Feel better?" she asked.

"Bones," he said, moving his jaws from side to side. He turned back to the water, buried his head beneath it, then carefully lifted it with water trapped in his mouth. Throwing his head back, he gargled, then spit. The spray was like an uncapped fire hydrant. "That's better."

Janine spotted a couple of the lobsterlike critters shambling past. She tried to snatch one of them up with her beak. It slipped out, and she caught it in her claws. She popped it apart and munched.

"Ummmm," she said. "Needs butter, and maybe some Cajun seasoning, but I'll live. It's good. You should try some."

"Another time," Mike said.

"And these shells," Janine said. "I can think of uses for them, too. Hmmmm..."

Mike shook his head. "Can I ask you something?"

"Sure."

"How is it that you're coping with all this so well? I mean, one second you're at school, the next you're here, not even yourself anymore, but you seem okay with it. How are you doing that?"

"Hmmmm," Janine said. "I hadn't really thought about it."

That wasn't entirely true. She had a very good idea why she was able to handle this. But she wasn't in the mood for sharing.

"I think *you're* handling it really well," Janine said.

Mike's head bounced from side to side. Janine could feel the swell of pride radiating from him. She almost felt guilty. Complimenting him was a cheap dodge, an easy way to get out of talking about her feelings. But at least she'd meant what she'd said.

"Thanks," Mike said, then he grew still. He sniffed the air, and his dark eyes clouded over.

"What is it?" Janine asked.

"A couple of miles down the shore. See where the shoreline reaches inland? We can't see too much because of the trees."

"Okay," she said. "So, what's going on?"

Mike seemed transfixed. "We've gotta get over there. We've gotta do something!"

"Is it Bertram?" Janine asked. "Did he—"

"Now!" Mike growled, and raced ahead, moving so swiftly he was down the shore and out of sight before Janine could cover even a quarter of the distance.

She looked at her useless wings, wishing she could fly. Then she ran as fast as her legs would carry her.

CHAPTER 7

MIKE

The fear and blood that Mike had sensed on the southern stretch of shore had given him some idea of what he'd be facing. He told himself he was prepared. But he wasn't. Not for any of it.

On the shore, dozens of giant sea turtles had been laying their eggs. The turtles were a good twelve feet long and were mostly green, with streaks of yellow. Their shells were thick, rubbery skin, not horn.

They reminded Mike of leatherback turtles, with their friendly-looking hawklike beaks and big, paddlelike limbs.

The turtles were under attack—brutal attack. Their nests were being terrorized as well. The predators were tyrannosaurs, like him. Mike counted four on the shore. Three were his size, their flesh a mix of green and gray.

The fourth one, however, was a giant.

Mike stared with wonder. The giant looked twenty feet tall. His flesh was a deep forest green with black stripes. His eyes seemed to blaze crimson, but Mike suspected that was simply a trick of the light, a reflection of the terrible trauma the Tyrannosaurus had inflicted on the dying turtle at its feet.

The giant fell upon his victim, and Mike watched as he bit hard into the turtle's flank and tore open its shell. Then Mike turned away.

This was the natural order of things. The predators stalked their prey. It was as simple as that. Just like Sean always said. The strong survived, the others didn't.

Others meant kids like Lowell Kramer, the one player on their team whom Sean had identified as the source of their problems. Lowell was a little smaller, a little slower, a little weaker than everyone else on the team. He was also supposed to be the guest of honor at Sean's planned Big Event.

Mike shuddered and turned back to what was happening on the beach. Every now and then, a turtle would snap or bite at an attacker. But the T. rexes always leaped out of the way in time.

A roar came from the midst of the carnage.

The giant had seen Mike. He stared for a few moments, then went back to his feasting.

Around the T. rexes, dozens of turtles struggled to flee the beach for the safety of the water. Dozens more were trapped while still laying their eggs.

They were defenseless.

Mike Peterefsky knew that he was no longer in the twentieth century and no longer housed in a human frame. He knew what he was now. The meal he'd just consumed was still warm in his belly. Despite that, he was disturbed by the spectacle before him.

Inside, Mike was still human. His reaction was exactly what it might have been if he'd been on vacation, wandering on some beach, and had come across these monstrosities and their feeding frenzy.

Mike let out a fierce roar. He didn't think. He didn't agonize over it, the way he had about the Lowell Big Event. He just acted.

The giant looked up lazily from a new turtle he'd taken. He seemed amused by Mike. But he didn't stop. He ambled over to a fresh turtle and descended on it without missing a step.

The other T. rexes watched the giant. They

seemed to understand something in the same instant as Mike: The giant wasn't killing just what he needed to survive. He was progressing systematically through the turtles, wounding each severely, taking a small bite, a nibble, then moving on again. He wanted to make sure that as few as possible escaped.

He didn't *have* to do this. He just *wanted* to.

Mike couldn't believe what he was seeing. The other three T. rexes *could* believe it, apparently. They began to do the same thing. It was too much for Mike. He roared again, then broke into a frenzied run, right into the ranks of the turtles.

He didn't care that he had no idea how to fight in this body. It didn't matter in the slightest to him that all four of his enemies would have no qualms about killing him—or that they didn't seem at all worried about his approach.

Even the giant was nodding, as if in approval.

They think I'm coming to join them, Mike realized. If he'd been thinking more clearly, he might have used this to his advantage. Set some kind of trap. He could have planned it as if he were running a play during a big game.

But the only thing on Mike's mind was his anger.

"You're history," he whispered, intent on reaching the giant rex. He zigzagged through the turtles.

As he passed a smaller T. rex, an instinctual alarm went off in his mind. He disregarded it.

Big mistake.

A grunt sounded from behind him. Then came a host of strange noises.

My scent, Mike registered suddenly. *The other one is downwind of me now, catching my scent, and he knows, he understands I'm not like them—*

The second of the smaller green-and-gray T. rexes rose up before him, his maw opening wide as he tilted his head to one side and drove it forward with an unexpected swiftness!

My throat, he's going for my throat!

Mike reached up with his strong arms, hoping to grab hold of the oncoming powerhouse as if he were an opposing linebacker. His claws went up—

And didn't reach!

His tiny little arms weren't doing him a bit of good. He saw a blur of teeth, row after row of shining ivory incisors. He smelled the fetid breath of his attacker, sensed the heat of its body as it moved to take him in a single, terrifying embrace.

Mike tried to dive out of the way. It was something he might have done on a football field. But his new body wasn't built to handle the move.

His legs launched him forward with incredible power, but his head and left shoulder collided with the scaly tank barreling his way.

Wham! Mike was certain every bone in his body was going to shatter, every tooth in his skull was going to shake loose. Neither happened.

Instead, he heard the steel-trap chomping of the

other T. rex's jaws clamping on thin air as they both went down in a confused tangle, then fell away from each other.

Mike was on his back. The T. rex he'd collided with was still on the ground a few yards away.

One down.

Without losing a second, Mike flopped onto his belly and brought his legs up under him. He stood on the *first* try—just in time to confront a pair of new T. rexes racing toward him, one from either side.

Mike had very little time to think. A typical T. rex would probably stand still and target one of his two attackers. But Mike wasn't a typical T. rex.

He waited as the T. rexes were almost upon him, then he darted back, causing the two to collide, their heads smacking together with a sharp *crack!* The two growled.

All thoughts of Mike appeared to flee from them instantly. Their anger now was directed at each other. They bit and clawed, and butted and shoved!

Coach Garibaldi would be proud, Mike thought as he took a step back and bumped into something. He turned, expecting it to be a twelve-foot turtle.

It was the giant.

He roared, and Mike's reason dissolved. His fear became everything.

A second roar came, this one of challenge. Mike was stunned to realize that it had come from him-self—he had gotten in touch with his inner T. rex.

Primal Tyrannosaurus instincts issued a roar from Mike that said he wasn't backing down.

Suddenly, footfalls came from behind. The T. rex he'd stunned earlier was closing on him.

I've got to create a distraction, Mike told himself. *Think.*

Suddenly, he was dancing and hopping and banging his tail crazily on the ground. Then he waved his little claws and bellowed, *"Wahhhhhhhhhhhhhhhhhhh!"*

The giant froze. It stared at him.

"Wugga-wugga-wugga-wugga!" Mike hollered.

The footfalls behind him stopped, too. His distraction had worked on *both* T. rexes!

The giant roared. His head lunged forward, jaw snapping just inches in front of Mike's face. He took a step back, keeping his tail up so that he wouldn't trip over it. The giant matched his stride.

Mike took a few more steps backward, turning so that he could see both his adversaries at once. Behind them, the other pair of T. rexes was still engaged in a savage ballet of tooth and claw.

Mike knew he was outmatched. This was an enemy he could not fight. Not *fairly.*

A mad jumble of ideas and images flooded into his mind. A few weeks ago, Mike had been assigned a Sherlock Holmes story for English, and he'd liked it so much, he'd gone out and bought all the Sherlock Holmes books.

A scene from one of the coolest stories came to him: Sherlock Holmes fighting Professor Moriarty. They were locked in a mad dance of death, about to tumble over Reichenbach Falls. The falls. The water...

He thought of Janine. The way she had warned him not to wade deeper into the water.

Out of the corner of his eye, he saw the turtles scurrying into the water, where they'd be safe. *Why?*

Mike decided to find out. Darting to one side, he faked out Moriarty—the giant T. rex, the pack leader, his enemy.

Mike raced for the water. His rex instincts screamed at him to stop. Not in words. Just in a gnarled feeling in his gut that told him this was *wrong*.

He ignored it.

Thunderous footfalls sounded behind him. Moriarty and his henchman were closing in. The shore was dead ahead. Mike pictured a goalpost at the edge of the water. One yard. Two—then a great splash as the water rose up around him. He felt its chill on his feet. His legs. Up to his thighs.

He waded in deeper, his tail flashing and splashing! The water rose up to his belly and began to engulf it. He took another step, sinking deeper into the frothy waves, and turned to look behind him. Moriarty and his henchman were at the edge of the shore, staring at him in disbelief!

"Come on in, the water's fine!" Mike shouted

deliriously. "Come on, ya big wussbags! Come on, show me how tough you are!"

Moriarty grunted. His companion grunted. They came a little closer, stepping tentatively into the lowest threshold of the waves. Then they stopped and would go no farther.

"Wimps!" Mike shouted. "Wussies! Cowards!"

Moriarty and the other T. rex just stared at him.

Suddenly, Mike felt it. He looked down and finally understood why Moriarty and his pal hadn't followed him: He was *sinking*.

The soft pull of the sand was yanking him down. He tried to take a step forward, but the beach was swallowing him up, like quicksand! It was because he *weighed* so much! Tons! "Oh, no..."

Moriarty and his minion turned and stomped back down the shore toward their interrupted meal.

"No!" Mike shouted. He drove himself forward, but he only sank deeper. Mike became aware of other shapes in the water. Swimming quickly, and with purpose. Sharks. While on the shore, Moriarty drew close to another defenseless turtle, his maw opening wide.

Enraged, Mike thrust his head into the water and closed his teeth around the body of a shark that was about to bite his tail. He yanked it out of the water, whipped his head sharply, and sent the flailing shark flying in the direction of his enemy. The shark glistened as it wriggled and soared through the air.

"Catch that pass!" Mike hollered.

The shark smashed Moriarty right in the face. Moriarty snuffled and sneezed. His companion let out a loud, disgusting sound that might have been a burp but sounded disturbingly like laughter!

Moriarty turned and growled. Then he charged into the water!

Now what? Mike thought.

He braced himself as if the league's biggest linebacker were on his way. There was no one to receive a pass, and no time to run. Moriarty was on him in a heartbeat, teeth flashing, a savage roar bursting from him.

The giant rex crashed into Mike, the impact sending them both hurtling farther into the water. As they struggled, bit, and clawed at each other, bubbles rose around them.

Mike tried to hold his breath, but Moriarty was all over him, tearing and slashing.

Then something struck them! Mike caught a brief glimpse of a dark shape, some kind of leviathan with monstrously huge fins, curling and moving in the water. The impact separated him from Moriarty. He tumbled end over end into the murk surrounding him. Flailing and kicking, his lungs aching, he was certain that he would drown here.

A streak of crimson passed before his eyes. He looked beyond it and saw Moriarty with his maw sunk deep into the flank of the sea monster that had struck them. Then a wave rushed at Mike, striking him hard, sending him back toward the shore!

Mike saw the bright glow of the sun on the sur-face of the water above, then sank again. His feet struck something hard, a stone buried in the sand, and he vaulted off it, propelling himself up and for-ward. The surface seemed to thrust itself at him, and his head burst from the water! He gulped at the air greedily, his lungs on fire, his little arms pistoning, though they did him no real good.

A wave crashed down upon him, driving him clos-er to shore. His head escaped the water, but when he kicked at the sand, his feet sank. He was trapped again!

"Here!"

Mike flinched as something splashed into the water in front of him. It was long and heavy, with a pair of rocks tied to one end of it. Bertram's tail!

Mike used the last of his strength to open his maw and snag the club at the end of his friend's tail, and he kicked with his feet. Suddenly, the hungry sand released him.

He was free!

As he broke the surface, he sucked in air without letting go of Bertram's tail. He could see the club-tail laboriously pulling him forward.

As they reached the hard-packed sand of the shore, Mike let go of Bertram's tail. Shivering, he took a few steps. Out of the corner of his eye, he saw a shape coming toward him.

Moriarty!

Mike was so startled he allowed his tail to get tangled between his legs. He fell onto the shore, belly-up, helpless prey, just as Bertram had been.

Moriarty stepped forward onto solid ground. He lunged toward Mike's stomach—and Bertram's tail whipped out, smashing Moriarty in the mouth!

"No more!" Bertram hollered.

Moriarty's head slapped to one side, shattered teeth flying. He stumbled as Bertram slammed him twice more. The giant fell—and got up again.

"We're dead," Bertram whispered.

But Mike had a feeling they weren't. An incredible splash sounded from behind Moriarty, and a beast out of legend rose from the water.

Surf, sand, shells, and tiny predators fell away from the dark round humps of the creature's body. Mike saw on its side the ragged wound from Moriarty's attack. Then a long *neck* whipped upward.

Nessie, the Elasmosaurus, opened her maw and brought her head down upon Moriarty. Her snakelike neck whipped around the giant T. rex, and she dragged him toward her.

He kicked and roared, but she held fast, sinking back beneath the churning waves with a lazy, smugly triumphant ease. Moriarty thrashed about, but it did him no good. His body was hauled beneath the water. Then they were gone.

Mike wanted to cry out in relief and triumph, but

he knew there were three other rexes to worry about. He scanned the beach. A field of turtles was ambling toward the water. A few yards behind them, two of Moriarty's henchmen abruptly broke off their battle with each other and looked his way.

They sniffed the air, studying the odd pack of travelers who stood together. Shuddering, they loped off the other way. They were joined by the last T. rex, Moriarty's number-one guy, who appeared completely astounded at the loss of his leader.

"Our scents are confusing them," Bertram said. "They don't want anything to do with us. And they've fed enough."

Mike looked at the Ankylosaurus. "You saved my life. I don't know what to say..."

"Thanks would be good," Janine said. Candayce nodded.

"Thanks," Mike said softly. He felt weak, shaky, and ecstatic just to be alive!

Bertram seemed more engrossed in the sight stretched out before him. He walked up to one of the turtles. "Archelons. Cool..."

Mike shifted his gaze to stare at the pudgy little Leptoceratops. She was wearing *something*. Clothing? No, it was leaves, very large ones, and they were stuck to her body with sap or something. Two on her chest, one lower, like a bathing suit.

"Candayce? Are you all right now? What happened—?"

"I—I—oh, don't even speak to me!" Candayce snapped. "Let's just get out of here!"

"She's got a point," Bertram said, turning away from the turtle. "We've got a long haul in front of us if we're going to reach the Standing Stones in time."

"You know which way to go?" Mike asked.

"I've got an idea. We should follow the shoreline to the river, then head east to get back to Montana. Right now we're in South Dakota, and—"

"How do you know that?" Janine asked.

"Oh, God, here we go," Candayce moaned, plopping down on the sand.

Bertram's head bobbed. "The inland sea, the coal beds we passed, and...I just know. I can feel it. Mr. London really *did* bury a map in my subconscious. We're in what will become South Dakota. We have to head west. Follow the circumference of the earth..."

"I get it," Janine said. "When you move back in time, you also move in *space*. The earth is constantly rotating, so even though we didn't move, the world did. We ended up on the same latitude, but only—"

"Two hundred and forty-nine miles away," Bertram said.

"Yeah, just a little east of where we should have been dropped off," said Janine. "I guess it could have been worse."

"True. We could have ended up halfway around the world—or right in the middle of the ocean. Or we could have missed the earth's revolution around the sun completely and been left sitting in outer space," Bertram said.

"At least that would mean no one would see me like this," Candayce growled.

"I wonder what the future Mr. London's learned about—"

"Let's *go*," Janine said. "We've got to make almost thirty miles a day. That's not gonna happen if we stand around talking."

"Right," Bertram muttered.

Without another word, the small group turned from the shore. Mike looked at the turtles, many of whom would now be going home because of him. He felt good.

A sound came from somewhere far off. A Tyrannosaurus roar?

He looked back at the water. It was still. Moriarty was gone. He wasn't coming back. He *wasn't*.

Mike looked away once more, wishing he could believe that.

CHAPTER 8

BERTRAM

Night was falling. The sky was a deep, rich blue, with a dark purple band at its highest reach. Stars and the moon were out. There was enough light to see, but barely. All four travelers were winding down. Janine was sitting alone, working on some project. Candayce was with Mike and Bertram, rooting around in the sand among the large, beautiful shells.

"This is like summer in Florida," said Candayce. "My dad's an airline pilot. He's great, but he's not around much. Sometimes we go on trips. Anyway, everything's so different in Cocoa Beach. It's hot and humid; you can feel the air pressing in on you like it's got you in its wet hands...But at the beach, the winds are soft, the water's cool, the sun's like the best thing that's ever happened to you."

A sharp *pock* came from Janine's spot close to the water. Then a *caw* and a muttered curse.

"*What* is she *doing?*" Candayce asked.

"Don't worry," Mike said. "I'm sure it's nothing."

Candayce used her beak to pick up a large shell. "This one's good. Now I just need one more."

"You know what I wish?" Bertram asked.

"I can *imagine*," Candayce said.

"It's silly, but I wish there was a boardwalk. Someplace that sold hot dogs, Cokes, fries..."

"Uhhhh." Mike slobbered. "Don't do that to me."

"Me, either," Candayce said. "An all-veggie diet. Yuck."

"Sorry," Bertram said, lowering his head.

"Don't be," Mike said. "*I* could go for ice cream."

"*Ice cream,*" Candayce moaned. Bertram wasn't sure if he'd ever heard a more mournful tone.

"Yeah. With lots of nuts and crunchy stuff on top."

Candayce sighed. From down the beach came another *pock!* Then two more. *Pock! Pock!*

Candayce sprang to her feet. "What are you doing, you stupid social *reject?*"

Janine started to sing. "*My little buttercup...has the sweetest smile...My little buttercup...won't you stay awhile?*"

"She's impossible," Candayce snarled. Mike laughed.

Bertram looked down. "Candayce, be careful!"

"What?" Candayce asked, shifting to look at him. A grinding, crackling sound rose in the night. "My shell! Bertram, look what you made me do!"

Bertram winced. She'd ground it to dust underfoot.

"Sorry," he said.

"You should be!"

"Why?" came a fourth voice.

Bertram looked up to see Janine approaching. A strange sound came from her. *Cha-ching. Cha-ching!*

"Oh, no," Candayce whispered. "Not that sound."

Janine held something in her right claw. It was a collection of shells and hard platings from the "lobsters" they'd found. Holes had been poked through the shells, presumably with Janine's beak, and a vine had been run through the holes. It was tied at one end. The other end was for Janine to twirl. The *cha-ching* was the sound of the shells clapping together.

Janine had remade her key chain!

"I'm impressed," Bertram said.

"You would be," Candayce muttered.

Bertram smiled inwardly, delighted to be with Candayce, despite her terrible mood.

Candayce turned to Janine. "So, what were you saying?"

"*You* smashed the shell," Janine said. "Bertram was trying to warn you. You were making him apologize for *your* mistake."

"Actually—" Bertram began.

"I didn't make *him* do anything," Candayce said.

Janine whipped her chain. *Cha-ching!* Candayce froze.

"Well, if you couldn't make *him* do anything, how could he have made *you* do anything?" Janine asked.

Candayce stared at Janine, chest heaving, her beak trembling as if she were desperately attempting to come up with some reasonable answer.

"Losers," Candayce said finally. She turned her back on Janine and resumed looking for shells.

Janine watched her for several seconds. "You want to do a Little Mermaid here, don't you?" Janine asked.

"Go ahead," Candayce said. "Mock me."

"Her leaves fell off," Mike said. "The sap dried out."

"I can help," Janine said. "Find your shells. I've got more vine."

"What?" Candayce asked.

"I'll help."

"Liar." Candayce found Janine staring at her. Bertram knew that look. Even in the body of a Quetzalcoatlus, Janine could look inside a person.

"Oh, gross! She's doing it again!" Frantically, Candayce tried to make the sign to ward off the evil eye, but her claws were too awkward for the task.

"Come on," Janine said. "Let me help."

"Really?"

"Yes."

Candayce and Janine went down the shore together. Mike and Bertram sat quietly. They heard Janine and Candayce talking, heard a shriek of glee, then heard a couple of *pock*s!

"Can I admit something to you?" Mike asked.

Bertram was surprised. "Sure."

"I'm scared. I'd give anything to, like, go over some rise and see a Blockbuster. Or a McDonald's."

"Me, too," Bertram said. "But we *can* do this."

"If we can keep from being eaten."

"Yes..."

"And if we can figure out the other thing we have to do, what Mr. London didn't tell us."

"We'll figure it out."

A scrambling sounded from down the shore. Janine came running. "You guys have to see this!"

Candayce raced to them and stopped, proudly displaying herself. On her chest was a makeshift brassiere, a pair of shells tied together with a vine. Another shell was draped beneath her belly. It was the most absurd and yet strangely comforting sight Bertram had ever beheld.

"Finally, a little bit of civilization!" Candayce said.

"I like it," Mike said.

"Me, too," Bertram agreed.

Candayce went prancing down the beach. Janine said, "Being back here does have its moments."

Bertram finally laughed. He looked to the midnight blue of the sky and the sparkling stars that were brighter now. In the morning, they'd be at the river, and soon after that...who knew? But eventually—and he prayed it would be in time—they'd reach the Standing Stones.

What would this world have done to them by then? he wondered.

P
A
R
T

T W O

Scales Are a
Fashion Disaster!

CHAPTER 9

CANDAYCE

Candayce Chambers was dreaming. In her dream, she was lounging on a deck chair, and her bathing suit had attracted the attention of a half-dozen guys around the pool. They stared at her long, beautiful legs, her tiny waist, her flowing golden hair.

Their girlfriends glared, but Candayce didn't mind. She reached back and stretched, enjoying the bold warmth of the blazing sun. Heat radiated through her. She lapped it up like a hungry kitten.

She was a goddess and she knew it.

Opening her eyes, she felt a momentary confusion as the dream fell away and she was confronted by the sight of star-shaped palm fronds high above. She followed the leaves down to a fat trunk decorated with diamond-patterned bark. The tree was ten feet high, and it leaned a little to one side. But...there weren't any trees near the pool. What was this?

She felt a cool breeze upon her bare chest.

Bare?

Candayce sat bolt upright, her arms moving to cover her chest: She was sitting on the edge of a pond, being gawked at by a group of slack-jawed dinosaurs!

The dinosaurs had fat bodies, parrotlike beaks, and little crests for foreheads. They were about six feet long, and most were dirt brown or stone gray. Two had purple-and-gold streaks and splotches. Another was emerald. To Candayce they were utterly repulsive—but at least they were keeping their distance.

"Good dinosaurs," Candayce whispered. She wondered if any were behind her, or if she could just turn and make a run for it. Only one way to tell...

She spun, her brain commanding her body to bring her long, sleek legs up under her. She imagined the whole thing in a heartbeat: how her legs would piston, how she'd launch herself to safety.

It didn't happen. Instead, she fell over onto her side, her tail caught between her legs. Tail?

Candayce looked down at her scaly body. She screamed—for all the good it did her. She was a Leptoceratops. Just like her admirers. No amount of hollering was going to change that.

She screamed anyway. The other Leptoceratops tilted their heads. They made odd clicking sounds among themselves. A few touched tails.

Candayce stopped screaming. She kept *doing* this to herself. Three long days now in the Late

Cretaceous, and she couldn't even begin to get used to this new and stubby little body she'd been given.

She looked at her "admirers." The Leptomaniacs weren't trying to hurt her. In fact, they had maintained a respectful distance.

She surveyed the ground, trying to find the bikini top Janine had helped her to fashion out of shells. It was gone! It'd been important to her to keep herself covered, even though a part of her knew that it was a pointless gesture. There was nothing left to cover up.

"All right," she said. "What do you losers want?"

The Leptomaniacs didn't answer. Couldn't answer, of course. They didn't understand English. And Candayce, even though she was in the body of a Leptoceratops, couldn't speak Leptoceratopsese.

Two of the group broke off and planted themselves on all fours. The first put his head down. With a loud chuffing and a series of shrill cries, he charged a tree!

Candayce watched as the Leptomaniac bashed himself into the weird leaning palm—and brought it down! The tree fell with a terrible thud. Then the second Leptomaniac launched himself at another tree. There was a sharp crackling, and the tree toppled.

This one collapsed only a dozen feet off to Candayce's left. A few of its branches fell within a yard of her. The sight of the rich green leaves was too much for her. Though she couldn't quite believe she was doing this, Candayce went on all fours to the branch and gobbled up a couple of leaves.

They were *delicious*.

Out of the corner of her eye, she saw the second Leptomaniac ram his shoulder against the flank of the first. As she ate, she studied this second one closely. He had a little scar on his chin, kind of like Harrison Ford. The first one had dreamy, soulful eyes, like Brad Pitt. Not bad, not bad...

It occurred to her that she was feeling some kind of attraction for each of these guys at exactly the same time she felt something *crawling* around inside her mouth.

There'd been a bug on one of the leaves! One of those real big ones!

Eeeeeeeoooooouuuuuuuggggghhhhh!

Candayce choked, and spat out the leaves, shaking her head and collapsing with an inner sob.

She *hated* it here. She just wanted to go home!

A chuffing came again. The Bradster was ramming his shoulder into Han Solo's flank.

This is what she'd found cute just a moment before? Gross! What could she have been thinking?

It came to her: *It's not what you're thinking, it's what the dino you're inside is thinking.*

Too weird.

She rose up on her hind legs. No way was she going to walk on all fours. Especially not in front of these guys.

All the plain-looking Leptoceratops got on their hind legs, too. Candayce froze. They froze. Oh, no.

This was bad. She'd seen this kind of thing before.

A third Leptomaniac, this one a bit more portly than the others, broke from the formation. With a running leap, he toppled another tree. The tree crumpled and sank to one side. Candayce was convinced it was going to come down right on her!

Turning, she ran a few feet and stumbled on a rock. A shadow came crashing down upon her. She didn't have time to scream!

Then she heard a great splash and felt a spray of chilly water cover her dumpy little body. She looked up and saw that the tree had fallen into the pond separating her from the Leptoceratops clan.

Suddenly, a dozen Leptomaniacs were all around her. They made cooing sounds of concern. A few snatched branches from a nearby tree and tried to dry her. They seemed nervous, yet excited to be so close to her.

She had *definitely* seen this behavior before.

Candayce stared at the Leptomaniacs ringing her in. Brad and Han were at the front of the crowd. The portly one was in the back, his head down. A few of the others jostled him. The brightly colored Leptoceratops stood close to the rear of the group. Strange high shrills erupted as they moved their heads from side to side, their beaks clacking.

Candayce rose and took a step back from the group. She held her head high. It was as dignified a pose as she could muster.

"I'm going now," she said, hoping that she sounded calm and in control. "I'm going, and I expect each and every one of you to stay here. Is that clear?"

Candayce took another step. Her companions gave her room. A few chuffed. One actually sniffed her.

She tried not to think about that.

Instead, she kept backing away, moving slowly.

As she withdrew, she watched the faces of her companions. They doted on her every move.

Candayce Chambers knew what they desired. She'd dealt with it before. They wanted her to be their queen.

CHAPTER 10

BERTRAM

Bertram was just waking up when Mike came thundering through the clearing they had chosen as their "camp" the previous evening. His Tyrannosaurus body made the ground shake and the diamond-shaped leaves of the nearby Williamsonias quiver.

Mike opened his mouth and spat out some fish.

"For me?" Janine said. "You shouldn't have."

Bertram watched as Janine unfurled her wings and yawned. In another time, he might have been fascinated to study the actual manner in which a young Quetzalcoatlus yawned.

Not today. He sank down on his haunches and closed his eyes, wishing he could sleep a little longer.

"Come on!" Mike growled. "We've been doing great the last three days! A good twenty-five miles a day. That's terrific. But today, we're going to do even better! So, wakey, wakey, rise and shine, come on in, the water's fine!"

Bertram was in no mood for this. His tail swung

102

lazily from one side to the other. He opened his eyes and looked at Janine, who was finishing her meal.

"Come on," Mike cheered as he wandered off and started doing deep knee bends, "we've got a lot of distance to cover, and we need to get *to* it!"

Janine shook her head. "Who put the batteries back in the bunny?"

Bertram looked at her. "Huh?"

"It keeps going and going..." she joked.

Mike finished his exercises and looked around. "Candayce took off again?"

"It's what Leptoceratops do," Bertram said absently. "They sun themselves in the morning, soak up the energy from the rays to get them going."

Mike gazed up at the open space visible through the trees. Bertram automatically did the same. Sunlight streamed into the clearing. Soft, gentle breezes drifted by. It was a little chilly, not unlike New England in late spring. Sweater weather. But nice. Certainly not the hot, steaming, soggy weather any of the others said they'd expected in the Late Cretaceous. Bertram had explained that this environment was seasonal, and while they wouldn't get snow, they were heading toward the cold season. This morning, the sun's warmth was welcome.

"She could have sunned herself here," Mike said.

Janine shrugged. "Guess she doesn't like the scenery."

Mike sighed. "Somebody's got to go get her. Janine?"

"That's my middle name," Janine said. "*Somebody*. This is the third time in a row I've been *Somebody*. It's time for someone else to be *Somebody*."

"Candayce won't argue. She's scared of you."

"True," Janine said, springing to her feet and walking with a bounce in her storklike step. She snatched up her key chain and whipped it back and forth, *cha-ching, cha-ching*.

Bertram knew Candayce hated that sound and would know Janine was coming. And be afraid.

Janine went off in search of her prey.

Mike looked over. "I'm gonna go study that bark while the ladies are away. I suggest you do the same."

"I went already." Bertram felt a sudden flush of anger. "I mean, I know I'm just a moseying, slothful creature, but I *do* remember to take care of things without having to be reminded."

"It was just a suggestion." Mike put up his claws. "All right, then."

Bertram watched Mike go deeper into the woods and shook his head. *I should have been the T. rex.*

All his life he'd been an Ankylosaurus. Dull, plodding, yet powerful—in his intellect, at least. But in other ways, he'd been unable to catch up. He was the one people had to protect, never the one who was admired. It just wasn't fair.

Of course, none of this had been his idea. Sure,

he'd built the machine that had transported them to the Late Cretaceous and dumped them into the hulking frames of dinosaurs. Fine. He was guilty of that much. But he hadn't done it on purpose. That the machine had attained miraculous powers was purely random, a trillion-to-one shot. If he *had* planned for it, he would have put himself in the body of the T. rex.

He still could recall when he'd been five, out walking with his dad, and he'd go into Tyrannosaurus mode. His eyes would glaze over. He'd sniff the air for prey and walk with his hands held close to his chest, three of his fingers tucked in, the other two tapping together like the two-fingered claws of a confident, alert T. rex.

His dad had always smiled at this. He would say, "You've got a sense of wonder, Bertram. That's the most important gift any of us could be given. Don't ever be ashamed of it. Don't ever run from it. Just enjoy it."

Then, even if they were in public, his dad would drop onto all fours and wave his butt in the air, shouting, "I'm an Ankylosaurus! I'm lunch if you can catch me!"

And they'd chase each other, and laugh, and be happy.

I should have been the T. rex.

"Heads up!" Janine called from a few hundred yards away. "Incoming!"

Bertram turned and saw Candayce barreling toward

him. A pack of Leptoceratops was chasing her.

"Help! Help! Help!" Candayce demanded.

"Get on top of me," Bertram said.

Candayce stopped dead. "Yeah. In your dreams."

He shook his head. *"Climb* on *top* of my *shell.* Look *out* for the *spikes.*"

"Jeez, you don't have to be so—"

"Now!"

Candayce scrambled up Bertram's shell. He saw a few of the Leptoceratops go down on all fours, as though they were getting ready to spring at him. Oh, right. That would be smart.

Bertram raised his tail and brought it down hard. The ground shuddered.

"Whoa! I almost fell!" Candayce yelled.

"So be more careful," Bertram muttered. "Or deal with these guys yourself."

"Okay, okay," Candayce said. "Jeez. What *hasn't* gotten into you?"

Bertram moved in a circle, smashing his tail to the ground in warning. The Leptoceratops withdrew to a safe distance.

"I can still see them," Candayce said.

"Get off me, will you?"

"Right. Sure. I—wait!" Candayce exclaimed. "What's this?"

"What?" asked Bertram.

Candayce stepped down, stomping on the back of Bertram's head in the process.

"Hey!" he yelled. "That hurts."

"Good," Candayce said, holding something in her claws that clacked and banged. "Don't look at me!"

He turned away, though he had no idea why she had asked him to.

"All right. You can look now."

Bertram turned back to find Candayce holding her shells before her.

"Do these look familiar to you?" she asked.

"Yeah," Bertram said. "What about them?"

"You might have noticed that I wasn't wearing them when I ran to you, asking for help. I was *naked!*"

"Candayce, we're all—"

"My shells were hooked on one of your spikes! You stole them from me when I was sleeping!"

Bertram had no patience for this right now.

Janine approached, slapping her shells. *Cha-ching.* "Hey, Candy Striper. Want me to tie those?"

Mike appeared from the woods. "I heard all the noise. What happened?"

Bertram nodded toward the Leptoceratops pack, now quaking at the sight of the T. rex.

Seeing the pack's fear, Candayce moved over to Mike. "Hey, this is more like it," she said.

Mike looked down. "What's with the shells?"

In her most sultry voice, Candayce said, "Zip me up, dear."

"Huh?"

"Just tie it," she hissed.

Mike went to work on tying together the lengths of vine. He fumbled for a while, but Janine helped.

When it was done, Candayce leaned against Mike. "I know I can trust *you* not to pull any funny stuff."

Mike looked at the club-tail. "What'd you do?"

"Nothing," Bertram replied.

"Then let's get to walking," Mike said.

They set out on the path Mike had cleared for them the night before. Fallen Pityostrobus, sixty-five-foot conifers, and pine cones lined the path on both sides. The pack of Leptoceratops trailed behind them, scrambling between the trees. Bertram barely noticed. He watched how closely Candayce stuck to Mike.

"Figures," Bertram said. He wondered what advice his mom might give right about now. The last time he'd seen her was before she took off for San Francisco and that "Limited Awareness Seminar," where she met Fred the Real Estate Guy and didn't come back.

Janine came running up to him. *Cha-ching, cha-ching*. "Hey, sunshine!"

Bertram sniffed the air. "Actually, I think there's a storm front coming in."

Janine shook her wings. "Why ruin things while we're behind, right? Let's make it a flash flood."

"Flash floods happened a lot in this era," Bertram said glumly. "I don't see why it wouldn't be possible."

"I know why you're so crabby."

"Really?"

"Sure. I know a lot of things. Like these trees,

they're 'pity-ohs'—or, in your case, 'self-pity-ohs.' But it's not the flora that's got you down."

"It's not?"

"Nope. It's the lack of fiber in your diet. Actually, it's the lack of *anything* in your diet. You haven't eaten. At all. Not since we got here."

Bertram tensed. "Just not hungry."

"It's been days."

"Not...*hungry*. What part of that didn't you understand?"

"I think it's more than that."

"Really?"

She bobbed her head. "I've *read* about Ankylosaurus. I know what happens when they eat."

Bertram's tail whipped out so sharply he smashed a nearby tree into twigs. Janine danced out of the way, nearly dropping her chain. *Cha-ching!*

Mike and Candayce looked back. "You two okay?"

"It's nothing." Bertram sniffed and looked back at Janine. "Did you steal Candayce's shells?"

"No. Wish I could take credit, but sadly, no."

"Then who?"

A *caw* sounded from above. A second Quetzalcoatlus was flying overhead. "Loki!" Janine called.

The Trickster bowed his head, sailed in a lazy circle, then flew off.

"Loki?" Bertram asked.

"You're changing the subject," accused Janine.

"You *named* him?"

"Hey, if Mike can name his, I can name mine."

Bertram shook his head. "Nessie. Moriarty. Loki. What's next? The Grinch?"

"You're still changing the subject. I know your secret, Bertram. If you don't eat something soon, you're going to slow down even more."

Bertram panicked. "What should I do?"

Janine looked around, her tiny claw scratching her chin. "How about...*eat something!*"

Bertram looked up to see if Mike and Candayce had heard her. They were about a hundred feet ahead and lost in a conversation of their own.

"You have to," Janine said. "We both know that."

"Not necessarily," Bertram said. "There are theories that many dinosaurs could eat huge meals and store them in their bellies and slowly use up that energy—"

"If your body was digesting, we'd know it," Janine said. "It's not. That means you need to eat."

Bertram felt like he wanted to cry. "Come on! Isn't this humiliating enough? Walking on all fours? Being as wide as a car and as fat as—"

"A car without any fuel ends up on the side of the road. I don't want that happening to you."

"You don't?"

Janine shook her head.

"I guess I gotta do it sometime. It's probably why I've been so short-tempered. So irritable."

"Probably."

Bertram waddled off and went to work on a low-hanging branch.

"Hold up, everyone!" Janine called. "Chow break!"

Mike and Candayce stopped. They didn't wander back. They were completely engrossed in their talk.

Bertram hated to admit it, but he felt jealous. He knew the kind of person Candayce was. And in this body, she was hardly a beauty anymore. Still, there was something about her that made his heart race.

He chomped away on the leaves, ignoring the twigs he snapped up and crunched. It was delicious! He'd almost never tasted anything so good! He had no idea exactly how hungry he'd been!

"Bertram!" Mike called sometime later. "Come on, we need to get going!"

Bertram shook himself. It was as if he were waking from a dream. He saw that he had grazed through four trees and over a dozen bushes and shrubs. He'd even knocked down a couple of thirty-foot-tall Araliopsoides to get at the leaves. And the greens from the ginseng trees had been very tasty indeed. As he munched, he'd become unaware of any action but eating. Freaky. But he did feel better.

Suddenly, he became aware of sounds from all around. "Company," Bertram warned.

"It's the Leptos," Janine said. "They never really left. Now they're all around us."

"Hey, guys, don't worry about it," Bertram said. "I think I know a way of getting rid of them."

"You're kidding," Candayce said. *Really?*

"You bet," Bertram said, exchanging a sly glance with Janine. "You bet."

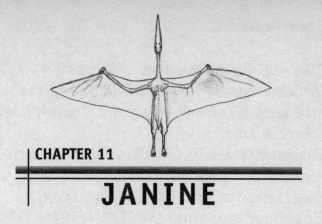

CHAPTER 11

JANINE

Bertram's plan took effect about an hour later. One moment, the group was ambling down the "dirt road"; the next, they were under attack. Only the attack didn't come from without. It came from within. Within *Bertram,* to be exact.

"What'd somebody step in?" Mike hollered.

"That *smell!*" Candayce wailed.

Janine glanced over at Bertram. He looked as though he wanted to drag his head inside his shell like a turtle. Then a strange thing happened. He held his head high and began to lecture them.

"The digestive process of an Ankylosaurus is different from a human's. It's similar to that of rhinos, horses, cattle—"

Brrrrrrrrrrrr-UPPPPPPPT!

"Was that what I thought it was?" Candayce said.

Mike was looking unsteady. "That wasn't a fart! That was the queen mother of all farts!"

"I'm afraid I'm just getting started," Bertram said.

"Oh, no!" Candayce wailed.

Janine smiled inwardly. She didn't like the stink, but she knew it couldn't be avoided. "Hey, it's not all bad. Look around."

Janine gestured to the trees flanking them. The pack of Leptoceratops was running for cover.

"See, Candayce? Bertram did you a favor!"

Brrrrrrrrrr-rrrrrrrrrr-rrrrrrrrr-UPPPPPPPPPPPPT!

Janine had seen Bertram's backside wiggle before the last one and moved upwind.

"You see," Bertram continued, "because my frame is so large, parts of my insides are separated into special compartments. Bacteria living within my stomach serve to break down woodlike materials within the fermentation chamber and—"

"It's not bad enough you're the little geek who got us into all this," Candayce wailed. "No! Now you have to hit us—"

BRRRRRRR-UPPPPPPPPPPT!

"Ugh!" Candayce wailed, teetering.

Bertram lowered his head shamefully. "Sorry."

"You should be!" Candayce hollered.

Janine had seen enough. She used the tip of her beak to snap the vine that was holding Candayce's shells on her ugly little body.

"Hey!" Candayce cried, trying to catch the shells. Janine snatched them.

"Catch me if you can!" Janine sang as she ran ahead into the woods. *Cha-ching, cha-ching!*

The brush beneath Janine's feet nearly tripped her a few times, but she managed to reach the top of a rise before Candayce caught up with her.

"Give—them—*back!*" Candayce demanded.

"Oops," Janine said, tossing the bikini top over the rise. Candayce watched as her shells fell hundreds of feet and smashed on a rock.

"Fine," Candayce said, her hooves covering her scaly, flat chest. "I'll just get some leaves and glue 'em on with sap again."

Candayce turned her back to Janine and started hunting for leaves.

"Excuse me," Janine said.

Candayce ignored her.

"Hey, *butt-face!*"

The other girl turned. "What did you call me?"

"You're the one who turned around."

Candayce chuffed. She lowered her head.

"That's right. Drop to all fours and try to knock me down. Just forget you're the most popular girl in the eighth grade and start acting like a butt-faced dinosaur. That's what you are, after all."

Candayce looked down at her plump little body. Her shoulders sank. Her head dropped onto her chest. "I am," she said at last. "Aren't I?"

"A butt-face, you mean?"

Candayce raised her hoofed claws. "Just *stop.*"

"When are *you* going to stop with Bertram?"

"Huh?"

"Bertram. The one with the crush on you."

Candayce was startled. "He's got a...on me?"

Janine nodded. Candayce began to laugh. It was Janine's turn to be startled.

"It isn't funny!" Janine whipped her chain. *Cha-ching!*

"Oh, this is going to be *great!*" Candayce shrieked. Her guffaws caused her entire body to quake.

"Bertram's a decent guy," Janine said. "You'd better not—"

Candayce screamed and giggled. "Entertainment! Oh, thank you, finally, some entertainment!"

Janine stared as Candayce giggled like the cruel little witch she'd always been. Janine knew her mistake. She'd tried to appeal to Candayce's good side. She'd assumed such a thing existed.

"My mistake," Janine muttered. She moved forward, slapping her chain. *Cha-ching!*

Before Janine could reach Candayce, the trees at the edge of the clearing shuddered. There was a harsh crack, and a tree toppled off to their left. Another crack, and a tree sank down to their right.

A second later, the pack of Leptoceratops burst out of the woods and came charging their way. Janine eyed the nearby precipice. The drop was sharp. Dangerous. She pictured the pack accidentally driving Candayce and herself over the edge.

Instead, the gang came to a thundering halt and ringed in Candayce. "Um...Janine?" Candayce called.

Janine tried to think of what she could do. Though her wingspan was incredible, her body was hollow-boned and scrawny. The Leptoceratops, on the other hand, were like mini-van versions of Triceratops. Smaller and without horns. But still strong.

Janine looked to the sky, hoping to see Loki. The sky was sleet gray—and empty. The Leptoceratops ringing in Candayce moved closer. They nudged her. Firmly.

"What do they *want?*" Candayce cried. Janine tried to get closer, but two of the plain-colored Leptoceratops turned and shot fierce growls her way. Janine let out a high *caw* that startled them.

Including, unfortunately, Candayce.

Janine sighed. "You were supposed to make a run for it. I was trying to give you a diversion."

"I didn't know! How was I supposed to know?"

The portly Leptoceratops flung himself at Janine. She sidestepped, and he flopped to the ground. Several of the other Leptoceratops bobbed their heads and shoved at one another. Their tails lazily slapped on the ground.

Candayce suddenly sprang into action. She vaulted forward, aiming herself at a breach between two of the Leptoceratops. She made it through.

Then four more Leptoceratops rose up and moved in upon her, gently but firmly butting her flank and driving her to the ground.

"That's it!" Candayce cried. She got up, her claws

flashed, and she whacked herself.

"Oww," Candayce murmured. Shaking her head, she tried to kick with her stubby little legs. And fell down.

Don't hurt yourself, a petty and very pleased voice deep within Janine's head whispered. Then the seriousness of the situation impressed itself on her, and Janine felt ashamed.

"What are you doing?" Janine asked.

"Defending myself," Candayce hissed.

"It looks like you're falling down."

Candayce got up again. This time she used her head as a weapon. She targeted a reddish-colored Leptoceratops and rammed its left shoulder. It stared at Candayce quizzically.

"Clavicle, knife-edge strike!" Candayce screamed. She turned, oblivious to the lack of effect her move seemed to have had upon her intended victim. She lowered her head, hooked it in front and beneath the jaw of another Leptoceratops, and brought it up sharply. This dinosaur's head slapped back. He tottered for a moment, and fell.

"Palm heel underneath to chin!" Candayce barked.

This little move did not go over well. The Leptoceratops crowded in on Candayce. Janine tried to get close, and two Leptoceratops rushed her. Dropping her chain, she scratched at them but somehow hit Candayce instead, raking the vine that held on her bikini bottom. The shell fell away and was ground under the feet of other Leptoceratops. Then a bunch were in Janine's face, driving her back to the edge of the abyss.

With a shrill cry, Janine fell into the waiting arms of nothing at all. A part of her sensed that this free fall was the most natural thing in the world for her to experience. Then she panicked. Her body flipped over and she saw the ground rushing upward. *Open your wings, stupid! Do it!*

She spread her wings and was surprised as she caught an updraft. The thermal carried her a hundred feet above the ground in a graceful arc. The feeling was exhilarating. She was flying!

She turned back in the direction of the drop and angled her wings just a little, and she started to rise.

An earthen wall approached. It was the hill she'd fallen from. She heard a rush of air and tried to *will* herself higher. The wall slapped her. The impact made her skull ring. She felt herself falling again. She screamed and clawed for a handhold. Anything that might save her!

She found it. Her claws became entangled in roots clustered on the side of the earthen wall. Hanging there, she hollered until Mike and Bertram arrived. Bertram hung his tail over the edge and Janine carefully transferred herself to it. He hauled her up and she sank to the ground, hugging it dearly.

"So where's Candayce?" Mike asked.

BRRRRRRRR-AHHHHHHHHPTTT-PLLLLLUHPPPPHHH!

The noxious smell made Janine cough. "The Leptoceratops..."

"No!" Bertram whispered. Candayce and the Leptoceratops were gone!

Janine helped Mike scan the ground for tracks. He couldn't use his nose to find Candayce; the smells Bertram was manufacturing had taken that particular sense out of the equation.

They found a confusion of tracks, new and old, and paths that led off in a half-dozen different directions.

Janine shook her head. "You'd think we'd hear her calling for help."

"You'd think," Bertram said. He looked guilty—and worried. "How far could they have taken her? We'll find her. I know it."

Janine picked up her fallen chain. *Cha-ching!* She considered letting Bertram know that she'd told Candayce about his crush on her. But the club-tail was in such a bad state she decided not to.

Janine didn't feel very good about the position she'd put Bertram in.

If she could fly, really fly, then finding Candayce—and scouting the locale of the Standing Stones and the best route to them—would be easy. What she needed was some flying lessons.

Again she looked to the sky. But Loki was nowhere to be seen. "All right," Janine said. "I'll just have to figure it out for myself."

CHAPTER 12

CANDAYCE

Candayce was being carried. She was on her back, up in the air, a half-dozen Leptoceratops walking in tight formation, shouldering her weight equally. She rocked gently, her tail drooping, her view of the world shaky and upside down. She saw trees. A forest. That meant she could be *anywhere*.

She wasn't sure how long it had been since the Leptomaniacs had grabbed her. But it was getting darker. She couldn't tell if that was because the storm was coming or because it was getting late.

Think, she commanded herself. *You get sluggish at night. Are you feeling sluggish now?*

She was, but that might have been a result of having been knocked cold. *So, try something else.*

"MIIIIIIIIIIIIIIIIIKE!"

The Leptomaniacs scattered. Candayce fell to the smelly ground with a thud. A group of ratlike things scampered off with little squeals. Candayce picked herself up, her heavy feet crunching on a carpet of beetles. Butterflies whipped past her. The air was thick with bees.

Candayce glared at her captors. She had no idea why they were doing this. Had she jumped into the body of the clan's princess or something?

It was possible, she supposed.

"Mike, can you hear me!" she hollered. A strange baying sound left her lips. The other Leptomaniacs imitated the sound. They could hear, but not understand, her mental cries to her friend. This other noise appeared to have some meaning for them.

Candayce waited. No Mike. Didn't he care?

Or was he so far away that he couldn't hear her call?

Candayce forced herself to calm down. Mike would come for her.

She looked around. The Leptomaniacs had taken her to a sparse forest that was lit by the vanishing sun. The light fell upon the vine-covered oaks, dogwoods, magnolias, and ficus, making them shimmer like gold. The shattered remains of tree trunks were all around her. The ground was moist.

The body of a large, long-necked dinosaur lay dead ahead. Candayce had never seen so huge a creature in her life, never even imagined she would. It must have been close to seventy feet long. And here it was, lying on its side, the life drained out of it.

She felt saddened in a way she rarely acknowledged. She felt bad not only for herself and her lost opportunity to see this creature in the full of life but also for the long-neck. Some hidden history deep within her brain told her that the days of the long-necks were drawing to a close. Staring at the creature, she wondered if it had died of loneliness.

A chuffing came from behind her. Candayce realized that the baying had ceased. The Leptomaniacs were closer now. And very attentive.

"I don't care if you can understand me exactly or not," she said. "I'm gonna talk, and you're gonna do what I say. Understood?"

The plain-skinned Leptomaniacs hung on her every word. They were the males. Suitors. Candayce was sure of that. The colorful ones, the females, stared at her angrily but made no move to stop her.

"Now," Candayce said, "I want you to take me back. My friend Mike will be looking for me. He'll be angry if it takes too long to find me. You don't want that." The Leptomaniacs stared at her. "Mike. The T. rex." They looked at her adoringly. *All right,* she thought, *charades. That'll work.*

She started mimicking Mike's tyrannosaur movements, trying to get her point across. The Leptomaniacs imitated her imitation. It made her realize it wasn't a very good imitation to start with. No wonder they had no idea what she was talking about.

"Okay," she said. "We'll go to plan B. I'm walking out of here, and no one's stopping me."

She took a few steps before the Leptomaniacs

crowded in on her. She couldn't believe this!

"Leave—me—*alone!*" she bellowed. The Lepto-maniacs looked around, trying to understand where her voice was coming from, or so Candayce imagined. It gave her an idea. She thought of a car horn honk-ing. She played the memory of it in her head at a deafening volume. The Leptoceratops darted about, panicked.

"Oh!" Candayce cried. "Didn't like that one, huh? How about this?" She sent a bullhorn and a police siren into their minds. The Leptos started mashing into one another.

"Don't like it when you're not in control, do you?" Candayce said. She looked to the females. They were worried, but not as much as the males.

Candayce would have to do something about that. She considered Mike's T. rex roar. That would make them show her some respect.

GRRRRRR-ROOOOWWWWWRRAHRRRRHHHH!

Candayce shuddered. She hadn't made that sound. The roar came again. Closer this time!

Relief spread its wings inside her. "Mike!"

Thunderous footfalls came from the trees behind the Leptomaniacs. The ground shook.

"Mike, just a little farther, here I am!"

GRR-AWWWWWWHHHHRRRR!

Weird how he wasn't answering her calls. She looked at the Leptomaniacs. "You think I'm going any-where with you people, well, you're crazy!"

The brightly colored females huddled near Candayce while the males surrounded them, each facing the direction of the threat. They were making a stand.

A tree shattered into a rain of splinters, and a wobbly T. rex appeared. His flesh was sallow. There was a madness in his eyes. It wasn't Mike.

"Oh, no," Candayce whispered. Terror gripped her, and she wailed, *"MIKE!"* at the top of her lungs, praying that somehow he would hear her.

The T. rex grunted in annoyance and came for the group. The Leptomaniacs held their ground.

Roaring, the T. rex stopped before them. He sniffed the air. Once. Twice. Again.

By the tyrannosaur's scent, Candayce could tell it was an old T. rex. Two hundred years, maybe. Vision blurred. Senses dulled. And the Leptoceratops had it in them to put up a real fight.

The rex looked past the group to the carcass of the long-necked dinosaur. Without a backward glance, he shambled toward it and began his feast.

Candayce stared at the Leptomaniacs in wonder. She thought about the way they had taken her. "It had something to do with Mike, didn't it? It's not natural for plant-eaters to be hanging out with predators. You thought I was being kept for food. Or I was crazy or something."

She stared at them in shock. "I get it. You were trying to protect me!"

The Leptoceratops did not reply. Yet they seemed to sense a change in her. This time when they walked on, they didn't force her to come with them. They left the decision to her.

Candayce considered remaining on her own. Then she looked back to the old T. rex, who was savaging the long-neck's remains. She'd be safer with the group.

Hours drifted by as she followed the Leptoceratops. Finally, they entered a lush valley. Candayce was startled by the sight of *hundreds* of Leptoceratops. They milled about, separated into small groups.

I wonder which are the popular ones, Candayce thought.

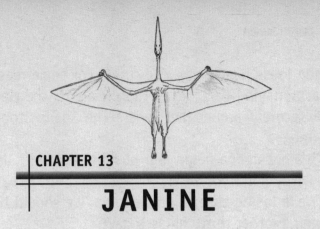

CHAPTER 13

JANINE

The earthen wall rushed toward her. Janine pulled up with her wings, knowing full well that she was going to hit it, and hit it *hard*.

The impact rattled her. Janine fell back, wings spread, and tumbled to the flat ground. She landed staring up at the purple streaks of twilight peeking through the dense black clouds. The dwindling sun was a blinding streak on the horizon. A rumbling came. Mike and Bertram made their way over to her.

"Hey, that was good!" Mike said.

"You think so?" Janine asked. Her voice held an undercurrent inching toward sarcasm.

Bertram's head poked into view. "You flew for thirty seconds that time."

"I managed *not to fall* for thirty seconds," Janine corrected.

"There's a difference?"

Janine knew that there was. She climbed up the small rise, determined to try again. Her chain was coming loose. *Cha-ching, cha-ching.* For some reason, it was annoying her. Rather than leave it, she tied it more securely around her wrist. The shells stopped clacking.

"It's not gonna help, your pushing yourself," Mike said. "Why don't you rest?"

"We're losing time," Janine said. "We should have covered another thirty miles today."

"It's not your fault," Bertram called, a slight tremor in his voice. "You couldn't have stopped it."

She hated the way Bertram sounded. He was blaming himself for what happened to Candayce.

Janine trudged up the incline. She'd sent herself off from thirty feet last time. She reached the mark she'd made in the dirt—her tag from her graffiti days. She climbed another ten feet, then unfurled her wings.

"I'm not worried about whose fault it is," Janine said. "I'm...never mind."

Janine didn't want to explain herself. They might not understand. This whole flying thing was about more than trying to rescue Candayce. In fact, if it weren't for Bertram's feelings of guilt, Janine wouldn't have minded *never* finding that little witch.

Each time she'd soared today, Janine had felt freedom and a sense of peace unlike any she'd ever known. Her refusal to give up had nothing to do with guilt or her stubborn resolve not to let anything beat her. She was doing this for herself.

"Can't give up," Janine said. She felt as if she were close to a breakthrough. If only the Quetzalcoatlus within her would cooperate. This body *knew* how to fly. But it wouldn't give up its secrets.

Janine launched herself, her wings straight, her stomach again leaping into her long throat.

Rrrrrrrr-crrrrrrrwwwwwwhhhhrrrrrr?

Janine fought the urge to look up. She'd found that the position of her head made a difference in her flying. Besides, she knew who it was. Her heart thundered with excitement. It was Loki. The Trickster.

"Nice one with Candayce's shells," she said.

Her fellow Quetzalcoatlus soared before her. For an instant, his wings were so close, they obscured her view. She saw a flash of gold, with hints of azure and crimson, then the colors streaked beyond her field of vision. It was like staring into the sun and quickly looking away, the image burning in your vision for a few seconds before fading. Incredible.

Keeping her head straight, she looked down and saw Loki soaring toward Mike and Bertram.

"Hey!" the T. rex yelled. It came out as a roar.

The Quetzalcoatlus turned and dropped his feet. For a second he hung there, wings unfurled, suspended in midair. Then he was driven up and back. He looked like a parachute that had opened suddenly, catching an updraft.

Janine watched, fascinated, unaware of her own actions. Reaching out with her right claw and drawing back an equal distance with her left, she described a lazy circle over her friends.

Loki wasn't finished. He flipped over, then gracefully regained his dive-bomber pose. He caught another breeze and zoomed toward Bertram. He came within a foot of the club-tail and—

BRRRRR-AHHHHHPT!

Loki burped right in Bertram's face! Bertram's head was swaying slightly. He didn't seem to like the smell.

Janine giggled. She couldn't help herself. She couldn't remember the last time she'd felt like that! "Go get him, fish-breath!" she called. And without thinking, she sailed in a wide arc. She felt something. A wind. A strange undercurrent. A *thermal.*

She closed her eyes and allowed her body to drift into it. There was turbulence, and it frightened her, but only a little. She held on, and her body rose up and up...

She opened her eyes and gasped. She was a hundred feet over the land.

Whoa, what was I thinking! her mind screamed.

She heard a rustle of wings and saw Loki beside her. His head wiggled, and he made a sharp little *caw!* that made her smile. Her fear receded, and he stared at her, his dark eyes instantly arresting.

This is what you wanted, his gaze seemed to say, *so why are you afraid? Don't back down now. Let it go.*

Janine thought of the times late at night when she'd sneak away from the bed-and-breakfast her mother ran. She'd be alone in the streets with her gear stashed in her backpack. Her gaze would search the clean, smooth surfaces of buildings that hadn't yet been graced with her artistic prowess. She'd feel a near-mystical sensation as she pictured it as a canvas calling out to her for adornment.

That same feeling was with her now—only it was different. Better. Because the thrill that came to her in the middle of the night was gone—the thrill of knowing you were doing something wrong, that you could get busted. It had been replaced by the thrill of knowing she was right where she belonged and that what she was doing was the most natural thing in the whole wide world.

A wave of calmness settled over her.

She never took her gaze off Loki.

Her companion arced a little to one side. She followed. He moved his head and wings just a touch and rose a few more yards. She did that, too.

He dove abruptly, racing away from her, becoming tiny so *suddenly* that it took her breath away.

She didn't follow. Instead, she tried to lower her head and wings a few degrees, then a few more, but she was trying too hard. A surge of wind came at her, and she wasn't ready for it. The wind hit her like a balled-up fist, and she tumbled backward, spinning, falling—

A *caw* brought her back. She found the currents, and righted herself. Then she drifted slowly in ever-tightening circles back down to the ground.

She smashed into the earthen wall for another hard landing. Pain rippled through her. Looking up, she saw Loki soar into the skies. She studied his expression. He seemed annoyed at her for coming down, but this time he was willing to wait.

"I'm going up again," Janine said as Mike and Bertram came over. "Did you see me? Did you see?"

A tiny, far-off voice interrupted: *"Miiike!"*

Candayce's voice. Then it was gone.

"Did you hear that?" Mike asked.

Janine and Bertram nodded.

Mike turned. "I felt the direction it was coming from. I've got an idea which way we need to go."

"I'm with you," Bertram said.

Janine shook her head. "I'm not ready yet."

Mike appeared startled. "But you—"

"I'm not *ready*," she said firmly. "I need to practice more. Just go on ahead, I'll catch up before too long."

Bertram hesitated. "You were really something."

She nodded, feeling something she couldn't put into words. A strangeness about herself, her companions.

"Okay," Mike said. He turned and stomped off. "See you soon."

"Not if I see you first," Janine said coolly.

Mike looked at her.

"Just kidding," Janine said, though she really wasn't sure why she'd said that.

Mike turned and walked on.

"You should go ahead," Bertram said anxiously. "You can get there faster. I'll—"

"It's getting dark. We stay together."

Janine looked to the sky. Loki was still circling overhead. It occurred to her that she had never seen him on the ground. He couldn't stay in the air all the time. Where did he sleep? What did he like to eat?

She had more of a curiosity about these things than about where Candayce had been taken. A part of her felt this was wrong, while another part felt it couldn't have been more natural.

She climbed up the rise, reaching a hundred feet before she launched herself into the blazing sunset without once looking down.

CHAPTER 14

CANDAYCE

"You've made a mistake," Candayce said. A collection of brilliantly colored Leptoceratops stared at her with cool, unblinking eyes. Behind her was a group of very old, very sick, and very young Leptoceratops. Candayce had no idea why she'd been lumped in with them—unless they thought she was crazy.

"I have good reason for being with Mike," Candayce explained. "He might be a T. rex, but he's also the cutest guy in the eighth grade, and I'm by *far* the cutest girl. It's like a karma thing, you know? Our chakras are meant to merge, y'dig?"

Candayce realized she was mixing together things she'd read in a New Age book with a lesson from her sensei.

It occurred to her that she should have been listening more closely to what her sensei said in class. Maybe she should have been paying more attention to a whole lot of things.

Candayce looked around. The Leptoceratops'

"village" amounted to flatlands with a half-dozen small mounds bearing who knows what. That was it. Candayce figured that the mounds were important, because the "in" Leptos congregated around them. She'd tried to take a look inside one, but she'd been shoved away for her trouble.

"Okay, here's the thing," Candayce said. "You've seen the way those guys were drooling over me, right? That makes me a hot property. Like visiting royalty. You don't dump royalty in with the lame-os and old farts." She looked over her shoulder. "Nothing personal."

The Leptomaniacs conferred among themselves. They gestured toward the group with whom Candayce had been shooed and started making chomping noises.

"It's dinnertime, and..." Candayce began, trying to get their drift. "It's dinnertime, and you want me to eat with them. No, this is what I'm telling you, I—"

One of the Leptomaniacs charged Candayce, who was unprepared for the attack. All she saw was a flash of purple before being slammed onto her backside.

As she lay there, it occurred to her that she'd spent a lot of time like this lately. Knocked down onto her butt.

She didn't like it but decided to mask her displeasure. She slowly got up. Behind the females, some males were drifting over to see what was going on.

This is more like it, Candayce thought. *These guys will straighten out these stupid-looking cows.*

Two of the females stamped their feet and tails. The males retreated.

So much for that. Candayce gave up. "All right. I'll eat with the dweebs. What's for dinner? No, lemme guess—leaves! Right? We'll eat some leaves! And if we're really lucky, something gross and slimy will be crawling on them!"

The female Leptoceratops stared at her. They made chomping noises again.

"Fine," Candayce said. "You're all a bunch of vegetarians. Well, I'll tell you, where I come from, it's not easy staying on a veggie diet. You people have it made. Except for all the carnivores."

The female Leptoceratops gestured at the weak group behind Candayce, next at the forest in the distance, then made chomping sounds. Candayce took a long, hard look at the Leptoceratops behind her. They looked at her pitifully, the young with wide, teary eyes, the old with resignation and need, the sick with envy. They *all* were hungry. She could feel it.

"Well, what?" Candayce asked. "You can't expect them to get food for themselves. What are you waiting for?"

She found the gathering staring at *her.*

"Oh," she whispered. "You want *me* to get dinner for them. Like, I've got to prove myself worthy of joining the group. Like when some new girl wants to hang with Tanya and me. Okay, I can do that."

A trio of males pushed their way forward. Candayce recognized them. Han, Brad, and Bluto—the portly one. Candayce went to them, head held high. "Okay, guys. Don't get any ideas."

The females let her by. Candayce saw a healthy-looking grove of trees on the outskirts of the "camp" and pointed. One of the females butted her.

"Thanks," Candayce said.

Another moved to do the same. Candayce raised one hooflike paw. "Ahhhhhh!" she cried in warning. The second female stopped in her tracks. "One to a customer." The female looked to the others, who appeared equally clueless.

Candayce led her little entourage toward the outskirts of the valley, passing the well-guarded and mysterious mounds. A sudden memory of the giant turtles laying their eggs on the beach seized her, and she finally had an idea of what was going on here.

Tiny, vibrating chirping sounds came from the mounds. Candayce saw a little Leptoceratops poke his head over one side.

"Oh, how *cute!*" Candayce cooed. Then she caught herself. "In a ridiculous kind of way, of course. They're still a bunch of losers."

She walked with her posse to the grove of six-foot-high drooping horsetails and ferns with rigid feather-like branches. It occurred to her that if she were back in her own time she wouldn't wander off with three guys she barely knew. Her nervousness subsided when she saw their lovesick expressions.

"Okay, so time to get some," Candayce said.

The trio of Leptomaniacs came a little closer.

"Grub. Get some grub. *Jeez*."

Candayce used her beak to tear off low branches covered with leaves. She dropped them to the ground, starting a collection. The male Leptoceratops just watched. They were her escorts, Candayce presumed. Charged with the task of making sure she didn't run off. At least they weren't knocking down any trees in her honor. She could be grateful for that much.

Soon she had a pile of leaves so big she wanted to take a running leap and dive headlong into it. She hated to admit it, but this was actually fun. And those other Leptoceratops really *were* hungry—the old and sick ones and the little guys.

She wondered what it must be like not being able to fend for yourself. What if she had to depend on someone else for every little thing? The thought frightened her.

She heard a munching sound. Spinning, she saw Bluto and the others noshing on her spoils.

"What are you guys doing!" she yelled. She drove them off, hissing and spitting. They backed away sheepishly, mouthfuls of leaves hanging from their beaks. "No wonder they send the women to go get food. Men are babies, even back here. Nothing ever changes, does it? Jeez, why the heck do we girls ever think we need anything from you guys?"

Bluto, Han, and Brad exchanged worried glances. Lowering their heads and moaning, they opened their maws wide and spit out the leaves. Candayce couldn't help but notice that the leaves hadn't been chewed. There was no reason for it—a typical Leptoceratops had fifteen rows of teeth! But these guys had only held the leaves in their mouths, as if preparing to move them, not eat them.

Candayce looked at the pile she'd created, and wondered how *she'd* thought she'd move them. There really was only one way. "Oh," she said. "Sorry, guys. I get it now. You were trying to help."

The Leptoceratops stared at her blankly. Candayce knew she had to find a way to let the guys know it was okay to start hauling the leaves back to the hungry ones. Hmmmmm.

She picked up a mouthful of leaves and approached her companions. An expectant fire exploded in their eyes. Candayce realized the mistake she was about to make. She dropped the leaves. The guys looked sad and disappointed. Candayce sighed. If she had passed the leaves to any one of the three, that one would have been convinced that she was choosing among them.

Suddenly, all three surged forward, butting heads and shoving at one another to gather up the mouthful of leaves Candayce left on the ground. Candayce turned away. Her suitors would work it out.

She went back to gathering leaves. Her jaws clamped over a branch and closed on a dark sphere. A *squish* came from somewhere. Fruitopia!

A rush of flavor filled her mouth. Berries! They were delicious! Then she felt something on her face. She looked at her paws in the dwindling light. They were covered in the crimson goo from squashed berries.

Her thoughts flashed crazily on Tanya's mehndi tattoos. And on oddities like Janine, who made being rejected by one's peers an art form. Hmm. She took in her surroundings as if she were seeing them for the first time. The wealth of flowering plants. A rainbow of colors, of possibilities.

"Boys," she whispered, "it's time I dressed for the party."

Twenty minutes later, Candayce emerged from the grove. Her three stooges followed a considerable distance behind.

All activity among the Leptoceratops came to an end. All gazes were fixed on Candayce.

Candayce had never looked worse in her entire life—and she was loving it. She'd squashed berries to paint her scales red and purple. She'd mashed a collection of yellow, pink, turquoise, and emerald flowers into a kaleidoscopic paste that she'd mixed with sap and streaked all over herself. She'd glued flowers on her forehead and vines to her head. The vines dangled like dreadlocks and flopped into her face as she

walked. She was the biggest eyesore ever to walk the Late Cretaceous. It was an honor she cherished.

She danced through the valley, shaking her backside as she let the memory of a song ripple outward from her mind. She swayed. She sashayed. She spun around like a little kid. If this didn't make her suitors go running for the hills, nothing would!

Finally, Candayce reached the group of helpless Leptoceratops. She dropped her leaves near them. Brad, Han, and Bluto did the same. Candayce danced, throwing her head back, wiggling her hips, and shaking her dumpy, bumpy booty.

Suddenly, Candayce felt the earth tremble. She looked around just in time to catch two incredibly alarming facts. The males—every male—had come close. They were bobbing their heads, swaying a little with her dance, staring at Candayce with powerful interest.

And one of the females, the largest and most gaudily colored of the herd, was charging her.

Candayce yelped. She saw a blur of pastel green, sky blue, and banana yellow. Then she felt the impact! "Oww!" she yelped as she was knocked on her butt.

Staring up at the sky, she saw the first faint hint of stars. She heard the female turning and coming around again. Then a low growl and a chuffing sounded, and the female halted. Candayce got up slowly, achingly, and saw a male approaching. All the other males parted for this one. Candayce could guess why.

Candayce looked down at her crazily colored form and understood the terrible error she'd made. What was ugly to her wasn't necessarily ugly to these guys. Just look at *them*, she reminded herself.

She yanked off the vines, then dropped to the ground and rolled around as if she was having an attack. Dirt and herbs stuck to her, but she didn't care. The more, the better. When she was done, a small rainbow-colored dent had been left in the earth, and Candayce was back to her old self.

The female who'd charged her and the male who'd displayed interest were wandering away together, occasionally glancing back. She looked back to the old, the sick, the young...and sat down with them.

They stared at her, obviously grateful for the food she'd brought, which they noisily gobbled up. Burps, snapping twigs, chewing, swallowing, saliva dripping like water from a faucet. Candayce had some, too.

Brad and Bluto were still hanging around. Han had taken off. Maybe he was hungry. Or tired.

The sky darkened, and soon only the moon and stars provided any light. Candayce still could see her companions. At this point, she didn't care what clique she'd been tossed in with. Mike would come. Then this craziness would end.

She looked over at Bluto and Brad, and couldn't help but think of Bertram. Had he looked at her with that same kind of puppy-dog affection? Why hadn't she noticed? Of course, if she had noticed, she'd have made it worse for him. A part of her wondered why.

Staring at the boys, she decided it was habit. Whether it was a good habit or not, well...*whatever*.

A tiny warbling came from her left. Candayce saw a small Leptoceratops sitting alone, shaking. A few leaves lay next to the little guy, but he wasn't eating them. The others were looking at him.

"What's the matter?" Candayce barked. The small Leptoceratops jumped. He looked over his shoulder with wide eyes, then averted his gaze quickly. He was afraid of her. Too afraid to eat. And he needed to eat.

Candayce felt like a complete creep. No one had

made her feel quite as bad as this little *creature* had with that one fleeting look. She knew she had to do something.

She went to him on all fours. It was gross and humiliating, but something deep inside told her it was the right thing to do. The little guy looked up. His eyes were moist. They glistened in the moonlight.

"Don't be scared," Candayce said in her most soothing voice. She heard a coo from somewhere, a deep, lovely, warbling coo, and was stunned to find that it was drifting from her own beak. The little guy trembled. Candayce gently pushed a leaf close to him, then looked away.

Something tickled her side. The little guy licked at the sap and flowers still stuck to her. His tongue looked black in the moonlight. Berry juice.

"Ugh," Candayce whispered, "this is taking bonding a little too far." Candayce picked up the leaves with her beak and dropped them onto her legs. The little guy went for them greedily, biting and chomping, but never hurting her.

"Was it the dancing?" Candayce asked. "Is that what scared you so much?"

The munching Lepto gobbled away. Candayce felt a warmth spreading through her.

"Did you know I played the piano?" Candayce asked. She looked at her malformed claws. In her time, in her *body,* she had long, slender, perfect fingers. But here she couldn't play a note. Or could she?

Candayce closed her eyes and concentrated. A piece of music she'd never quite been able to master flowed from her memory. It was Chopin's *Raindrop* Prelude. She'd struggled so hard to learn the piece because she knew it was one of her mother's favorites, but she could never play it well enough.

It was a beautiful, luscious piece, moving, soft, like the raindrops for which it had been named. She'd never managed the emotions, the richness of it, never done it well enough to make her mom smile the way she had when she heard the piece when someone else, anyone else, played it.

This time it was different. Candayce wasn't just playing back a recording in her head. She was giving it voice with her imagination. She was playing the *Raindrop* Prelude, and playing it very well. It was everything she'd dreamed it could be.

The music drifted up from her soul. It blanketed the night. And for the first time since she'd fallen out of her body, out of her time, Candayce felt truly happy.

CHAPTER 15

MIKE

Mike and Bertram stumbled through the darkness. It had been a long time since they'd heard Candayce's cry. Mike wondered what had made her scream like that—and why they'd heard nothing since.

Sniffing, Mike tried to pick up her scent.

Nothing. Of course, his nose wasn't good for much. Beside him, Bertram gasped as another blast of exhaust fumes left his rear compartment. The stink was overwhelming. Mike kept telling himself that he'd get used to it, but he feared that he never would.

"Bertram, stop eating," Mike said.

"I haven't eaten since earlier today."

"Then stop—"

"I can't help it!"

Mike knew Bertram was telling the truth. He also knew that riding his friend over his indelicate condition wasn't going to help either of them.

His *friend?*

"I don't know if we're going in the right direction

146

anymore," Bertram said at last.

"I haven't known that for the last three hours," Mike said. "Make that four."

Bertram's fat elephantlike foot splashed, and water rose up around him. "Puddle," Bertram said morosely.

Mike took a step forward and splashed as well. "Big puddle."

Mike turned, took another step, and walked straight into a tree. "I can't see where I'm going. This is hopeless."

"It's not hopeless."

"All right—*we're* hopeless," said Mike.

"No we're not."

"All right, *I* am." Mike waited for a reply. "Feel free to contradict—"

"*Listen!*" Bertram whispered.

A light trilling came to Mike. The sound was unnatural. Hollow. A few tinny notes bouncing off one another in the darkness.

"Do you think it's Mr. London?" Mike asked anxiously. "Do you think he found a way to send us another message, or maybe a way to get us back—"

"Shh. Just listen."

Mike strained to hear more. The odd trilling sound increased.

"We must be near the river," Bertram said as they moved slowly forward.

"I think this *is* the river."

"Maybe. Dunno."

Mike heard the gentle gurgling of water flowing around stones. Bugs buzzing. Frogs. And that trilling. Mike looked around. "What's making that strange noise? That's what I want to know."

"Let's see if we can get past these trees," Bertram said. "If we can see the moon and stars..."

"Right."

As quietly as they could, they made their way around a half-dozen trees. Beyond them, they found—more trees.

"Oh, *man*," Mike growled in frustration, and he threw himself at one of the trees, snapping it. There was a crackling, then a whoosh of air as a portion of the tree splashed into the water. It triggered an eruption of movement. Thrashing. Strange calls. Scurrying. Then silence.

Bertram poked his head over the stump. "Hey, Mike?"

"What?"

"Clearing. Three trees down."

Mike followed Bertram to the clearing. He took in the stars shimmering on the surface of the rushing river. The water went right up to the tree line. Mike looked at the sky. Beyond the heavy veil of clouds, he could see the stars and the three-quarter moon. The trilling came again.

"There," Bertram said. "Look!"

Floating on the surface of the river was a pair of

eyes sparkling with moonlight. Mike saw them blink. One pair of eyelids moved up and down in a normal fashion, while a second pair closed side to side. Above the eyes was a lumpy forehead and a craggy crest that smoothed down into the water.

"Some kind of amphibian," Bertram said.

"Crocodile," Mike said. "Just a baby."

The little croc trilled. Somewhere close, his call was joined. Mike studied the water. It was brimming with life. Lowering his snout, he said, "Think I could go for a midnight snack."

"Hey!" Bertram cried.

"Not the croc. Look around." Mike pointed to the water. A school of fish swam around him. They were golden and looked like eels with fins.

"Ceratodus," Bertram whispered.

Suddenly, the baby croc darted at one of the eel fish and snatched it from the water. The fish struggled, slapping back and forth. Frantically, it whapped the croc on the head with its body. The baby croc's jaws opened, and the captive fish flew free.

"Here," Mike said to the croc, "I'll shove some your way." He dipped his head into the water, his maw open wide. He was beginning to enjoy trawling. He would savor this meal.

His snout bounced off something in the water. He pulled out, only a handful of fish squirming in his mouth. Perplexed, he chewed, crunched, swallowed. He wondered what he'd hit. The water *looked* deep.

Bertram gasped. The last time Bertram had gasped, it turned out to be a prelude to one of his killer gas attacks. Mike was in no mood for that.

The water rippled, and the baby croc started to rise. For a moment, Mike wasn't sure what he was witnessing. The baby croc seemed to be resting on something. Was it a sunken log? As he watched, more baby crocs came into view, wriggling and crawling over the rising thing. Mike stared at the "log." It had scales. A pair of glaring eyes. A snout. And teeth.

"Big mother—" Mike began.

"Yeah," Bertram finished.

The crocodile was—for a moment—as long and as wide as the river itself. Mike couldn't see the other bank. He couldn't see the end of the giant body. It stretched on and on.

"It's bigger than us!" Bertram said in an almost hysterical voice. "A lot bigger."

Mike didn't need to be told. The croc was at least fifty feet long, big enough to eat *him*.

"Run," Mike whispered. "Run—"

The crocodile leaped from the water, her offspring flying from her back, her jaws opened wide. Then she was on him! Her hot breath filled his snout with a mix of horrid stenches. Her jaws closed over Mike's head. Everything went black as he felt her teeth biting into the tough scales of his neck. Mike's little claws trembled.

Then he was falling headlong into the river. The

mighty grip of the crocodile's jaws tightened and pulled, straining to haul him downward.

Mike tried to open his jaws and bite as the water splashed around him. But there was no room inside the pressing depths of the croc's mouth. He couldn't breathe. And water was coming in fast, one second a chilling trickle, the next a freezing torrent.

He clawed and struggled and kicked. He whipped his tail. He sank.

Suddenly, explosions shook the river. One of the depth charges connected with the crocodile's body, and her hold loosened. Mike's claws found the soft underbelly of the croc. He dug in, hard.

The croc opened her jaws. Mike was free!

But water still surrounded him. He couldn't hold his breath much longer. His heavy body struck the gnarled roots of a gigantic tree. Then he saw something that sent slivers of cold steel into his brain.

A skeleton was tangled in the roots. A *tyrannosaur* skeleton.

He climbed onto the lowest part of the network of roots. He pushed with his powerful legs and drifted upward, his chest burning, straining. Then the moonlit surface came for him. His head broke free! Water poured from his snout. He climbed up out of the river.

Standing on the riverbank, Bertram yelled and cheered, his tail hanging over the surface of the water. It had been Bertram's club-tail that had provided the depth charges!

Suddenly, the water churned. The trilling rose to a fever pitch.

"Move!" Bertram cried. "Back away!"

There was a splash, and the big croc broke the surface. The trilling came again, and her young gathered on her.

Bertram looked over to Mike. "She didn't like us being so close to her babies, and she just plain didn't like *you*."

"Huh," Mike said. "You got all that—how?"

"She could've eaten you, Mike. She didn't. She wasn't hungry. You were lucky. *We* were lucky. How about we move our lucky backsides out of here? We know that the river runs east another twenty miles.

So, now that we've got our bearings—"

A brilliant light filled Mike's vision. Thunder sounded from somewhere close.

"Oh, *now* what?" Bertram asked. A curtain of rain struck hard. It came from nowhere. It was as if he'd been under a tent in a thunderstorm and someone had taken a knife to the roof, letting in all the water. The moon, which had been bright a moment before, was now buried behind thick dark clouds.

Bertram looked anxiously toward the river. "Oh, no. I was worried about this."

"What?" Mike said. He suddenly realized that all the mucking about in the water had cleared his nasal passages. His sense of smell was sharper than ever. He detected a bitter, acrid odor. Smoke? And a crackling electricity, similar to when Mr. London had sent his message. Similar—but not the same.

Lightning tore across the sky with skeletal fingers, two strikes from opposite directions that interlocked like joined hands. They faded.

"Whoa," Mike said. He looked to Bertram, who was waddling away as fast as he could. "What was it you were worried about?"

"Flash floods," Bertram said, moving as swiftly as he could. "They were common in this time period. The rains made the rivers overflow and—"

Lightning came again. It struck somewhere close.

The rain stopped as suddenly as it had begun.

"Freaky," Mike said. He took another step and

nearly tripped. Looking down, he noted a deep depression in the earth. A tyrannosaur track. Only this one was larger than any other Mike had come across. It was so big that it could have come from only one source.

"Moriarty," Mike said breathlessly.

"What?" Bertram asked.

"Nothing," Mike said. But that wasn't true. He'd had nightmares since the day the giant T. rex was taken out to sea by the Elasmosaurus. He'd dreamed that Moriarty had escaped and was stalking him. *These are old tracks,* he tried to tell himself.

"Mike, what's the matter?" Bertram asked.

"Nothing. Everything's fine," Mike said. For a moment, he wondered if he was just imagining all this stuff about Moriarty to give him something else to think about other than Lowell and Sean.

"So much for flash floods," Bertram said quickly. "And believe me, I'm glad to be wrong."

Mike turned to Bertram. "You know, back there, with the crocodile, I was scared. Weren't you?"

Bertram appeared deep in thought. Finally, he said, "Well, I didn't really have the time. Just trying to deal, that's all."

Mike laughed. "You're pretty amazing."

Bertram's head bobbed happily. "You mean that?"

"You've got more guts than I—"

A blinding flash of light made Mike freeze in his tracks. He saw lightning strike a tree a hundred yards to his right. A zigzag of pure destructive energy. A heavy branch toppled from above and fell in front of them. It was still smoking.

"Lucky it was wet. It didn't catch fire," Bertram said as thunder rumbled around them.

Mike sniffed. "It *did* catch fire," he said. "Look!"

In the distance, a reddish orange glow rose above the treetops.

"The Leptoceratops," Mike said. "I can smell them now." He nodded in the direction of the flames. "Bertram! They're right in the middle of the fire!"

CHAPTER 16

CANDAYCE

Candayce had been the first to realize what was happening. Lightning had struck a mile or so away, setting off a furious blaze. The Leptoceratops were racing into the woods, taking their chances with the fire that had all but ringed them in.

"There's nowhere to go!" Candayce yelled. "We have to stay here, we—!"

Lightning tore from the sky and struck the ground a half-dozen yards behind her. She felt its electric caress and understood why the Leptoceratops were leaving the valley.

She turned to them. "Okay," she whispered, "Come on, guys. Maybe we can find a stream or something to hide in."

They weren't moving. A few looked as if they were injured and *couldn't* move. The others were frozen with fear. Candayce screamed for help, projecting sirens into the minds of the Leptomaniacs to get their attention. But nothing worked!

"Jeez," she muttered. One minute she was *all that,* no matter what she did; the next she couldn't get arrested by these guys. She saw Brad and Bluto and decided to try one of the oldest routines on record. She put her hooflike claws to her jaw and swooned.

She hit the ground just as thunder shook the blackened sky. As lightning struck the far side of the valley, Brad and Bluto ran toward her.

"It's about time," she said. Brad went around her. Bluto tripped over her, then scrambled away.

Candayce sat up. "You—you—"

Thunder and lightning came again. One of the fleeing Leptoceratops screamed. Brad. He toppled over, smoking and twitching.

"No," Candayce cried. "No!"

But her screams did nothing to stop nature's fury.

She started to weep; then the words of her sensei emerged from her memory: *Pitying oneself is a form of theft. It robs you of action, and when you are in danger, action is oftentimes all that can save you.*

"Think," she growled. She looked to the helpless Leptos. Counted heads. Nine in all. If she had time, she could find vines, maybe fashion some kind of a litter to carry the sick. But there was no time, and her claws weren't dexterous enough for the task.

Lightning flashed. Closer this time. Candayce heard a shrill cry. Another Leptoceratops fell!

Options, she said firmly in her head. *Think of some options, blast it!*

She could nudge some of the helpless Leptos ahead of her, using music to calm the little one and get him to come along. That would save a few.

Or she could save herself. She didn't know why, but that *wasn't* an option, despite all the Leptomaniacs had done to her.

All they've done to you? And what is that? the voice of her sensei asked. *Made you face a certain aspect of your being? One that cares about the lives of others? That side has driven you all your life. But in all the wrong ways.*

"Hush," Candayce said. She had to think. Lightning struck nearby. Blinding, terrifying. Another cry!

Think! she demanded. *You're an A student. You know about lightning. You're not stupid. Think!*

Lightning always struck the tallest object. In the valley, the tallest objects were the Leptoceratops that were fleeing. Candayce scrambled toward the leftover Leptos. A few were sitting up.

"Get down!" she screamed. "Lie flat!"

When they only stared at her, she shoved them, butted them, flattened them one at a time, then held them down. Lightning strikes merged with the raging thunder. Every second felt like an eternity.

After a time, the space between the lightning and the thunder grew long enough to convince her that the danger had passed.

She was about to lift her head when the thunder returned. Only it wasn't alone. And *this* thunder was making the ground shudder.

Her heart sank as she realized it wasn't thunder. It was footsteps. Tyrannosaur footsteps.

She scanned the valley. That old T. rex was wandering around, scavenging on the Leptoceratops felled by the lightning.

Candayce remained still as she sensed the direction of the wind. It drifted across her from up near the rex. That meant he couldn't have smelled her or her little group. Good. So, now what?

A sound came from behind her. A shuddering wail. The old T. rex raised his head.

Candayce looked back. The cries weren't coming from her Leptoceratops. Suddenly, from one of the mounds where the young were raised, a few tiny heads poked out. A larger shape appeared behind the hatchlings and forced them down.

Fear knotted within her. Some of the Leptoceratops had stayed behind to protect the young, to shield them from the lightning with their own bodies. Candayce looked at the old rex. He wasn't paying attention. The cries came again, this time from a mound a few yards to the old guy's left, then from one way off to his right. The wailing rose ahead of him, behind him.

"No!" Candayce growled. "Stop it!"

The old rex lifted his head and roared, his dark

eyes reflecting the blazing forest fire beyond the valley. He turned and looked right at Candayce. She wondered, more calmly than she had any right to, if she could outrun him. It was worth a try.

He came for her. She willed herself into motion—but didn't move. Fear had been poured like cement into her bones, and she'd become a statue.

Just pretend it's Mike, she told herself. *This is just a game. A race.*

But this monster wasn't Mike.

Mike was kind and decent; he had honor and compassion. What was coming at her was dark, desperate hunger with gleaming teeth.

"Great," she whispered, watching the rex's jaws open. "*Now* I get some attention."

In another second, the rex would snatch her from the wildly shaking ground and devour her, or one of the defenseless Leptoceratops.

"You know what?" Candayce suddenly yelled at the T. rex. "I'm sick of this. The bugs. The stuff crawling on you, like, constantly. You guys roaming around like the biggest, baddest things that ever walked the face of the earth. I got one thing to say to you."

The rex was six feet away. His head reared up. There was madness in his eyes. Bloody anticipation.

Candayce loosed a sound from her memories, one she'd heard a hundred times before. A sound from the movies. A sound that her mind made as loud as it possibly could: "*SSSKREEEONKG!*"

Candayce watched breathlessly as the rex nearly tripped over himself, jamming his feet in the ground. He stopped, squinting, looking around, sniffing the air desperately for some sign of the monstrosity that made the near-deafening roar in his mind.

Godzilla rules, thought Candayce. Then she ran!

In seconds, the rex's curiosity was forgotten. He chased after Candayce as she raced across the valley. She heard the snapping jaws. She smelled his rotten breath and thought, *Pal, you don't have anything on Bertram!*

Her plan was to lead the old rex away from the young and the vulnerable Leptoceratops, and then—

She knew she'd forgotten something.

"Miiike!" she screamed.

No reply. The ground shook. The old rex was gaining on her. She studied the flaming curtain of the woods before her. It wasn't *all* on fire. She aimed herself at a blazing grove.

The old rex fell back a step or two. Candayce wondered if he might break off the chase altogether.

"Oh, no, you don't," she hissed. She had a plan. A crazy, stupid, suicidal plan, but it was *hers* and she wasn't going to let this jerk mess it up.

Candayce remembered the sound of the Leptoceratops' hooves crashing upon the ground. It was like a stampede from some old Western. She amplified the sound in her mind. Made it echo and shake. And sent it back at the old rex. He roared in delight! He thought there were dozens of Leptoceratops before him. With his poor vision he couldn't see them, but he could hear them.

Candayce nearly yelped with glee. She looked back. The rex chomped and snapped at thin air. Head down, he barreled forward, his hunger driving him. Candayce reasoned that he was too overwhelmed by his lust for food to care about the flames. But *she* cared.

The fires were before her now. She almost stumbled, her resolve and her legs weakening in unison.

Come on, Candayce told herself. *Mummy's always saying how thick-skinned you are, how nothing gets through to you. Let's see if it's true!*

She leaped into the blazing breach. Fiery branches crunched underfoot. The fern-covered ground was smoking, the path before her choked with black clouds. She felt the flames burn and sting.

Tripping on a tangled root, Candayce hit the ground. She saw the old rex charging through the blaze. He slammed into a burning tree, shattering it. The upper half of the trunk spun and fell. It nearly struck the old rex on the back but missed by inches. He charged toward her, the phantom sounds of the other Leptoceratops now gone.

Candayce turned and scrambled on all fours. Dignity didn't mean squat when you were being chased by a five-ton eating machine. And she needed to keep low to the ground, beneath the clouds of black smoke.

Flame seared her shoulder. She plunged deeper into the burning woods. Something smashed into her face, a cluster of fiery leaves, some brush, she wasn't sure what. She felt heat licking her cheek. She'd never been so frightened in her life. She ran faster.

Ahead, the forest was *melting*. Low-hanging branches were aflame like the sagging yellow-white remains of logs on a roaring fire. Shapes wavered. Blurred. The world was yellow, red, and white. She never believed anything could be so hot.

Smoldering embers fell onto her back. She hollered in pain but didn't stop. The thundering footfalls of her enemy rang in her ears. The flames were so intense that their roar was like the flow of water in a stream.

A stream. Water, cool fresh water. If only—

Crack! Snap! Candayce shuddered as a rain of branches and twigs struck her. The old rex was still coming. Candayce looked back to see debris bounce off his thick skull and shower down upon her.

Candayce coughed. Her breath was coming thick and labored. She slowed. So did the rex. But not by much. *Crack!* Candayce drove herself forward. She heard a loud crash behind her and turned to see the rex *dancing* with a tree. He'd slammed into it and was trying not to fall. He stumbled back, turned, and growled at Candayce.

He was injured, she realized. But still coming. She turned and ran.

Before her was an inferno. She couldn't see ten

feet. Flames ringed her at every possible juncture, but she didn't stop moving.

The rex's thunderous footfalls sounded: *Thud, thump, thud, thump*...

Then the ground quaked violently as the rex fell. The impact pulled the ground out from under her, and her head struck a smoldering branch with a sharp crack. She rolled onto her side and saw the rex lying like a fallen tree, black smoke billowing from his mouth and nostrils.

Nearby, sounds rose above the crackling of the flames—a series of high chatterings.

She heard a crunching of brush. Saw shadows, dark shapes coming for her.

"What?" she said hoarsely, the smoke clogging her lungs. She didn't think it fair that she was about to be consumed by some *other* predator after winning her race with the rex, not fair at all. But she knew that life was seldom fair.

Bluto came into view. Candayce tensed for an instant—then laughed! She laughed until she cried. Several other Leptoceratops crowded in, calling to her, nudging her to follow them. She felt something cool, a breeze.

Craning her neck, she saw a curtain of steam behind the other Leptoceratops. Water. *Of course.* They were in swampland. The flood plains.

She started to rise, and a growl came from behind her. She saw the blackened husk of the old rex picking itself up, opening its maw—and falling again.

Bluto squealed as the rex's wide maw sailed toward him. Candayce tried to move but couldn't. A shape pushed forward through the wall of mist. It barreled into Bluto, knocking him out of the way just in time. The purple female!

Bluto and the female fell in a tangle as the rex's jaws slammed down to the ground. The rex slumped, the energy drained from him. A tree trunk fell on him, pinning him where he lay.

Candayce stared at the rex. He wasn't getting up again.

She frowned inwardly at how, even for a moment, she'd once mistaken this creature for Mike. She missed him so much. Weird as it sounded, she missed all of them. Even Bertram and Janine.

Candayce followed the other Leptoceratops. They made their way toward a steaming lagoon. The waters were hot near the firmer ground, then cooler as she moved to join the other Leptoceratops in the center.

She collapsed, nuzzling another Leptoceratops.

The fire raged until morning.

CHAPTER 17

MIKE

Pale sunlight filtered through the skeletal forest. A soft, welcome breeze was stirring the thick, foul breath of destruction.

Mike and Bertram crashed through the woods. Smoke rose in lazy wisps from the remains of towering trees. Mike looked up as a sound came from above.

Cawwwwwwwwwwwwwww!

Janine soared above them, Loki at her side. Mike was amazed at the ease Janine displayed as she performed a figure eight in formation with her partner.

"Looking good!" Mike yelled.

"Up ahead," Janine called. "About a mile."

With that, she flew off. The second Quetzalcoatlus lingered, staring at Mike and Bertram with the slightly bemused expression that seemed permanently fixed on his face. With a rustle of wings, he departed.

"That was weird," Mike said. "Did you hear how cold she sounded?"

Bertram nodded. "Why do you think she's mad?"

"She might not be mad at all. Maybe she's just tired."

"Yeah, maybe..."

They trudged on. Since the previous night, Mike's sense of smell had been corrupted by the smoke that hung in the air. After losing the scent of the Leptoceratops, he'd gotten himself and Bertram lost. They'd stayed outside the forest fire but had been unable to sleep because of their concern for Candayce.

Janine's words had given them hope. Mike could see it burning in Bertram's eyes. Mike knew how Bertram felt about Candayce, no matter how badly she treated him. His friend would be devastated if anything happened to her.

Though exhausted, Bertram pushed on. Mike had to stroll so that he didn't pass him.

Soon they came to a valley that was alive with Leptoceratops. Many were gathered around mounds.

"You'd better stay here," Bertram suggested. "These guys aren't going to understand that you're not just a typical T. rex."

Mike knew Bertram had a point. He waited while the club-tail waddled ahead.

Candayce came running.

Mike was shocked at her appearance. She'd been burned in several places. It wasn't until she reached them that he could see her wincing with every move.

A few Leptoceratops followed her at a distance.

One was a little portly. Another was very young. The last one was a deep purple.

Candayce looked at them. She raised one claw, and waved. The Leptoceratops stared for a long time. The little one gave a heartrending cry and ran back to the group. The purple Leptoceratops reluctantly joined him. Finally, the portly one hung his head and made his way back to the others.

"Hi," Candayce said.

Mike noticed that her shells were gone. She no longer seemed self-conscious without them.

"Candayce," Bertram began, "your—"

"You're looking good," Mike said, whacking Bertram with his tail. If they made too much of the shells, Candayce might begin to miss them again.

Bertram appeared to catch on. "Yes, you are."

"I feel like crap," Candayce said. She looked at the soft pastel blue of the sky and the pale streaks of lavender and crimson. The sun burned above the horizon. "But it sure is nice to see daylight again."

Bertram's head bobbed in what Mike realized was blissful relief.

"We've lost time," Candayce said. "We're going to have to make it up. At least thirty miles a day, for starters."

Mike was stunned. "Um, right. That's right."

Candayce looked back at the other Leptoceratops milling around. A strange look entered her eyes. Mike wondered what it meant. Then it came to him. She was actually sad that she had to leave them.

"So, what happened?" Mike asked.

"They thought they were rescuing me from you guys," Candayce said.

"That's it?" Bertram asked.

Candayce nodded.

Mike was thoroughly amazed. He couldn't think of a time when Candayce wouldn't jump at the chance to talk about herself and her trials.

"Let's get going," Candayce said.

"Sure," Mike said, "but—where's Janine?"

Candayce looked around. "She's not with you?"

A sharp *caw!* came from above. Mike looked up, relieved. As two blurs passed overhead, Janine's "key chain" fell at Mike's feet.

"Janine?"

A pair of *caw*s answered him. Mike swiveled his huge head in time to see Janine and Loki soar over the trees and disappear from view.

"What just happened?" Candayce asked.

Bertram looked at the collection of shells lying on the ground. "There's something written on them!"

Candayce dropped down to all fours to inspect the shells more closely. "One of them says, 'Good luck.'"

Mike felt chilled. "What about that other one?"

Candayce looked away. "I don't believe this."

"What?" Bertram asked.

Stepping forward, Mike picked up the shells. "This other one says, 'Goodbye.'"

Mike looked to the skies once more, but there was nothing to see except a few soft clouds.

Janine was gone.

The adventure continues in

#2
THE TEENS TIME FORGOT
NOW AVAILABLE!

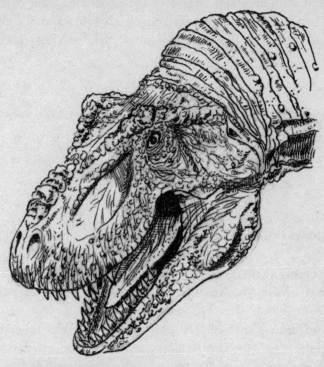

BERTRAM'S
NOTEBOOK

Ankylosaurus (ANG-kih-luh-saw-rus): One of the last armored dinosaurs and largest of the club-tails. Built low to the ground, Ankylosaurus walked on all fours and weighed three to four tons. Even Ankylosaurus' eyelids were armored!

Ankylosaurus

Carnivores (KAR-nuh-vorz): Meat-eating animals.

Cretaceous (krih-TAY-shus): The last of three distinct periods in the Mesozoic Era, 145 million to 65 million years ago.

Crocodilians (krok-uh-DILL-ee-unz): A sizable collection of reptiles that spawned modern crocodiles and other now-extinct creatures, some larger than any carnivorous dinosaur.

Herbivores (HUR-bih-vorz): Plant-eating animals.

Ichthyosaurs (IK-thee-uh-sorz): Water-dwelling, fish-eating, air-breathing reptiles.

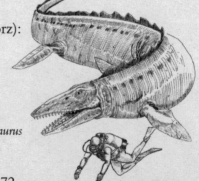

Ichthyosaurus

Invertebrates (in-VUR-tuh-braytz): Animals without backbones, like jellyfish.

Leptoceratops (lep-tuh-SER-uh-tops): The name means "slender-horned face." It was a Protoceratops of the same family as Triceratops. Leptoceratops was distinguished by its smaller size (the size of a pig), absence of horns, and beaked face. Leptoceratops was found only in North America.

Leptoceratops

Mammals (MAM-ulz): In the Cretaceous, they were small hairy animals.

Mesozoic Era (mez-uh-ZOH-ik ER-uh): The age of dinosaurs, 245 million to 65 million years ago.

Pachycephalosaurus (pack-ih-SEF-uh-luh-saw-rus): The name means "thick-headed lizard." These plant-eaters used their domelike heads for defense, ramming opponents with them much like present-day mountain goats.

Pachycephalosaurus

Paleontologist (pay-lee-un-TAHL-uh-jist): A scientist who studies the past through fossils.

Parasaurolophus (par-uh-saw-ruh-LOH-fus): Plant-eating crested dinosaur that was thirty feet long and stood sixteen feet high. Parasaurolophus' crest was a long, hornlike tube that curved backward from the head to beyond the shoulders and produced sounds.

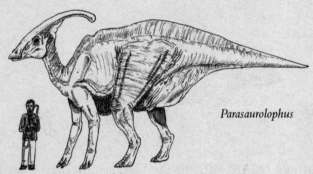

Parasaurolophus

Protoungulatums (proh-toh-UNG-gyuh-lah-tumz): Tiny mammals that were the forerunners of horses, antelopes, camels, and so on. They appeared to be part cat, part rat, and part horse.

Pterosaurs (TER-uh-sorz): Sizable and varied flying reptiles.

Quetzalcoatlus (ket-sahl-koh-AHT-lus): A pterosaur, a flying reptile that was not actually a dinosaur. A full-grown Quetzalcoatlus had a thirty-six- to thirty-nine-foot wingspan. It was the largest flying creature of all time.

Quetzalcoatlus

Triceratops (trye-SER-uh-tops): "Three-horned face." Triceratops weighed up to eleven tons and traveled in great herds near the end of the Late Cretaceous period in North America.

Triceratops

Tyrannosaurus rex (tye-RAN-uh-saw-rus recks): "King of the tyrant lizards," a large meat-eating dinosaur with tiny but enormously powerful arms, and muscular jaws filled with fifty teeth. Paleontologists differ on whether the T. rex was a predator who attacked live prey, a scavenger who lived on carcasses, or both.

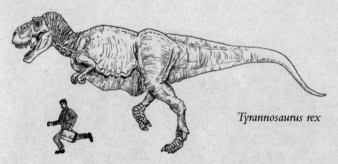

Tyrannosaurus rex

Vertebrates (VUR-tuh-braytz): Animals with backbones, like fish, mammals, reptiles, and birds.

The world: The continents and the seas of the earth 67 million years ago were different from those in our present day. North America was subdivided by an inland sea, and water also prevented movement between North and South America. Mexico was under water, India was a separate island, South America and Africa had begun to separate, and Europe and North America were moving apart. Seaways also divided Europe and Asia.

The World—Present Day

The World—67 Million Years Ago

SCOTT'S FAVORITE DINO SITES

(and Bertram has them bookmarked, too!)

DINOSAUR INTERPLANETARY GAZETTE
http://www.dinosaur.org
This site has *everything!* You'll find up-to-date information on the newest and coolest dinosaurs (check out DNN, the Dinosaur News Network), plenty of links, jokes, quotes, interviews with authors (like me!) and paleontologists, contests, and much, much more! The *Gazette* is the winner of 22 Really Kewl Awards and is recommended by the National Education Association.

DINOSAUR WORLD
http://www.dinoworld.net
A "nature preserve" for hundreds of awesome life-size dinosaurs, located in Plant City, Florida, between Tampa and Orlando. I've never seen anything like it! Check it out on the Net, then go see it for yourself!

DINOTOPIA
http://www.dinotopia.com
I'm the author of four Dinotopia digest novels, *Windchaser, Lost City, Thunder Falls,* and *Sky Dance. Dinotopia* is one of my favorite places to visit. This is the official Web site of James Gurney's epic creation. Enter a world of wonder where humans and dinosaurs peacefully coexist. Ask questions of Bix, post messages to fellow fans, and be sure to let Webmaster Brokehorn know that Scott at DINOVERSE sent you!

PREHISTORIC TIMES
http://members.aol.com/pretimes
This Web site offers information about the premier magazine for dinosaur enthusiasts around the world—published by DINOVERSE illustrator Mike Fredericks. For dinosaur lovers, aspiring dinosaur artists, and more!

ZOOMDINOSAURS.COM
http://www.zoomdinosaurs.com
A terrific resource for students. Lots of puzzles, games, information for writing dinosaur reports, classroom activities, an illustrated dinosaur dictionary, frequently asked questions, and fantastic information for dinosaur beginners.

#2

THE TEENS TIME FORGOT
by Scott Ciencin

Before the heavy rock could flatten Bertram, his tail whipped around and smashed it to pieces.

Mike was stunned—and impressed.

Head bobbing, Bertram looked over. "I got it, didn't I?"

"You sure did, but we better move," Mike warned.

Bertram trotted as fast as he could along the deep channel. Above them, the giant T. rex roared in frustration and rage, showering them with rocks whenever he could.

Mike decided he had to do something about that.

"Hey, butt-crack breath!" Mike yelled, waving his little arms and hopping in place. "It's me you want, stupid. Come on!"

The giant rex turned his attention on Mike, sending rocks down toward him. Mike darted and danced, only occasionally getting struck by the falling debris.

"You really think what I did was good?" Bertram asked timidly. "Smashing the rock with my tail?"

"It was incredible!" Mike wheezed. "If it was baseball season, I'd put you on my team any day!"

"You'd be the first."

"I mean it!" Mike dodged another oncoming rock. It exploded beside him.

Mike looked at Bertram's raised and swinging tail. Then he saw all the rocks lying about at their feet. "Hey, Bertram, how about a little batting practice?"

Bertram looked at him strangely. Mike grinned to himself. He used his small but immensely powerful arms to pick up a boulder. It was a good two feet around.

"Mike, what are you doing? He's still gathering ammo up there!"

"I'm the pitcher; you're up at the plate."

"What?"

Mike tossed the "ball."

Bertram swung! There was a sharp *crack*, and the rock became a blur. It smacked into the wall, leaving a small crater.

"Not bad!" Mike said. He looked up and saw the giant T. rex watching them uncomprehendingly. *Good.*

Mike found another rock. "You're a natural, Bertram. When we get back—"

"If we get back—"

"*When* we get back, you and me are gonna do some serious practicing, you got that?"

"*Really?*" Bertram asked.

"Darned straight. Here comes the pitch!"

Bertram's tail snapped forward and smacked into the rock at just the right angle. It flew up at the giant as if it'd been launched by a catapult!

The big rex had enough time to issue a slight grunt of confusion—and the rock hit him square in the forehead! He rocked back, legs buckling.

"We did it!" Mike yelled. "Home run!"

#3

RAPTOR WITHOUT A CAUSE

by Scott Ciencin

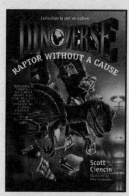

My name is Will Reilly, and I am a raptor. That's not how I started out. Three days ago, I was the most popular guy in Wetherford Junior High. No lie. I was the leader of the pack. Then some guy's science fair project went crazy and sent me back in time and into the body of this HUNGRY-HUNGRY-HUNGRY really hungry raptor. Trouble is, my new pack's not too happy with me. Not one bit...

BOOKS THE AUTHOR READ

Benyus, J. M. *Beastly Behaviors: A Zoo Lover's Companion*. Reading, Mass.: Addison-Wesley, 1992.

Bloch, M. H. *Footprints in the Swamp*. New York: Atheneum, 1985.

Czerkas, S. J., and S. A. Czerkas. *Dinosaurs: A Global View*. New York: Mallard Press, 1991.

Dixon, D. *Dougal Dixon's Dinosaurs*. Honesdale, Pa.: Boyds Mills Press, 1993.

Dixon, D., B. Cox, R. J. G. Savage, and B. Gardiner. *The Macmillan Illustrated Encyclopedia of Dinosaurs and Prehistoric Animals*. New York: Simon & Schuster/Macmillan Company, 1988.

Dodson, P. *An Alphabet of Dinosaurs*. New York: Scholastic, 1995.

Eyewitness Visual Dictionaries. *The Visual Dictionary of Dinosaurs*. New York: Dorling Kindersley, 1993.

Fastovsky, D. E., and D. B. Weishampel. *The Evolution and Extinction of the Dinosaurs*. New York: Cambridge University Press, 1996.

Glut, D. F. *Dinosaurs: The Encyclopedia*. Jefferson, N.C.: McFarland & Company, Inc., 1997.

Hanson, J. K., and D. Morrison. *Of Kinkajous, Capybaras, Horned Beetles, Seladangs, and the Oddest and Most Wonderful Mammals, Insects, Birds, and Plants of Our World*. New York: HarperCollins, 1991.

Horner, J. R., and D. Lessem. *The Complete T. Rex*. New York: Simon & Schuster, 1993.

Lambert, D. *Field Guide to Prehistoric Life*. New York: Facts on File, 1985.

Lambert, D. *The Ultimate Dinosaur Book*. New York: Dorling Kindersley, 1993.

Lambert, D., and Diagram Visual Information Ltd. *The Dinosaur Data Book*. New York: Avon Books, 1990.

Lessem, D. *Dinosaur Worlds*. Honesdale, Pa.: Boyds Mills Press, 1996.

Lessem, D. *Ornithomimids: The Fastest Dinosaur*. Minneapolis: Carolrhoda Books, 1996.

Masson, J. M., and S. McCarthy. *When Elephants Weep: The Emotional Lives of Animals*. New York: Bantam Doubleday Dell, 1995.

Norman, D. *Dinosaur!* New York: Prentice Hall General Reference, 1991.

Norman, D. *The Illustrated Encyclopedia of Dinosaurs*. London: Salamander Books Limited, 1985.

Retallack, G. J. "Pedotype Approach to Cretaceous and Tertiary Paleosols, Montana." *Geological Society of America Bulletin,* 106, no. 11 (1994).

Stanley, S. M. *Earth and Life Through Time*. New York: W. H. Freeman, 1989.

Walker, C., and D. Ward. *The Eyewitness Handbook of Fossils*. New York: Dorling Kindersley, 1992.

Wellnhofer, P. *Pterosaurs: The Illustrated Encyclopedia of Prehistoric Flying Reptiles*. New York: Barnes and Noble Books, 1991.

Wilford, J. N. *Riddle of the Dinosaur*. New York: Knopf, 1985.

• AUTHOR'S SPECIAL THANKS •

Special thanks to Alice Alfonsi, my amazing editor, and all our friends at Random House, especially Kate Klimo, Kristina Peterson, Craig Virden, Kenneth LaFreniere, Georgia Morrissey, Gretchen Schuler, Mike Wortzman, Artie Bennett, Doby Daenger, and Cathy Goldsmith. Thanks also to Denise Ciencin, M.A., National Certified Counselor, for her many valued and wonderful contributions to this novel. Thanks to Dr. Thomas R. Holtz, Jr., vertebrate paleontologist, Department of Geology, University of Maryland, for serving as project adviser, and to my incredible agent, Jonathan Matson.